2006

WHALE SEASON

ALSO BY N. M. KELBY

In the Company of Angels

Theater of the Stars:
A Novel of Physics and Memory

WHALE SEASON

A NOVEL

N. M. Kelby

SHAYE
AREHEART
BOOKS
NEW YORK

Published in the United States by Shaye Areheart Books,
an imprint of the Crown Publishing Group, a division of
Random House, Inc., New York.
www.crownpublishing.com

Shaye Areheart Books and colophon are trademarks of
Random House, Inc.

Library of Congress Cataloging-in-Publication Data
Kelby, N. M. (Nicole M.)
Whale season : a novel / Nicole Mary Kelby.
1. Recreational vehicle industry—Fiction.   2. Eccentrics
and eccentricities—Fiction.   3. Sales personnel—Fiction.
4. Florida—Fiction.   I. Title.
PS3561.E382W47   2006
813'.6—dc22   2005010836

ISBN 0-307-33677-8

Printed in the United States of America

Design by Barbara Sturman

2 4 6 8 10 9 7 5 3 1

First Edition

FOR THE JIMMY RAY WITHIN US ALL

ACKNOWLEDGMENTS

Many thanks to my wonderful editor Shaye Areheart; she is a great force for good in the world. Of course, I can never repay my friends and family for all their kindness, patience, and love; I am a handful at times.

Much chocolate and affection to my fellow writer Sue O'Neill for her invaluable copyediting help—and her spunk, too. I would also be remiss if I forgot to thank the Ragdale Foundation for providing a quiet space to begin this book; Poet Phil Memmer and the Downtown Writers' Center in Syracuse who honored me with a YMCA's Writers' Voice Fellowship so that I could finish; the state of Florida, for not only existing and giving me an endless bounty of material, but granting me an Individual Artist Fellowship in Literature to help pay my bills, and to the Atlantic Center for the Arts for awarding me the life-changing opportunity to work with Carl Hiaasen, a kind and decent man, who helped me find my outrage and humor again. And, always, to the wise and beautiful Lisa Bankoff—no finer, nor more fashionable, an agent ever navigated the MTA.

WHALE SEASON

Chapter 1

There are no whales in Whale Harbor, Florida. Never have been. The town was named during the Civil War as a way to lure Union soldiers looking for food and oil. It worked. So the name stuck.

But there are no whales.

Still, for many years, people came to whale watch. Some even thought they saw them. Blue whales, southern rights, humpback, killer, beaked, and beluga—as the subtropical temperatures rose, all manners of sightings, aided by tour guides offering free beer, were imagined in great detail. Written about in travel magazines.

But there are no whales.

Never have been.

This is why historians identify Whale Harbor as America's first tourist trap.

So those who come to this particular thicket of Florida's coast usually fall into two categories—the bushwhacked and the dreamers. Those who stay are both.

It's Christmas Eve and most of the town is at The Pink drinking eggnog schnapps. It's two for the price of one, in honor of the holiday. The jukebox is cranked, full volume. Jimmy Buffet asks, "How'd you like to spend Christmas on Christmas Island?" Nobody answers. Shot glasses surround hunched shoulders like picket fences.

The Pink's an all-purpose place. Up front, you can still buy bread and milk. Moon Pies, two for a buck. In the back, at the bar, you can still get your heart broken. Leadbelly whistles and jingles the blues. Christmas lights blink all year long across the tarpaper walls.

Right now, Leon should be there buying a round for Carlotta. She's been waiting for him for an hour, or more. Her tongue is white from the schnapps, and fuzzy. But he's not there. She looks at her watch again, the fourth time in ten minutes. Orders another round.

Bender pours the drinks in two deft streams. Schnapps arches like a waterfall. An impressive sight. Bender owns the place. He's also mayor. Hawkeyed and thin, in his early fifties, his spiky gray hair is dyed red and green for the holiday. It's a seasonal habit of his. At Easter, he'll go purple. He slides the two shot glasses in front of Carlotta. Tops them off with whipped cream and sprinkles that match his hair.

Carlotta looks up. "Thanks—"

And then he barks a noble clear bark. "Scottish terrier," he explains. Turns away before Carlotta has a chance to ask why he's impersonating a small hunting dog.

Most know not to ask.

Carlotta is new in town. She doesn't know anyone, but they all know her. At least, they know who she is: she's Leon's girl. That's the reason Sheriff Trot Jeeter is sitting three stools away and trying hard not to stare. But it is difficult. She's single. He's single. And, in the dim light of The Pink, Carlotta has a 1940s Veronica Lake kind of glamour. Boozy. Sultry. Bored. Her thick hair is carefully parted to one side, covers half her face. Trot can't take his eyes off her.

Of course, that's not surprising. He's forty-one years old. If he doesn't get married soon he'll have to get a dog— one that barks a lot. Scottish terrier sounds pretty good right about now.

The problem with Sheriff Trot Jeeter is not that he's unattractive. He's just unremarkable. Average height, average weight, average build—you couldn't pick him out of a lineup if you had to. Through the years he's grown comfortable in his absolute lack of distinction, the unnerving way he sometimes fades from memory while he's still in the room. And so, out of habit, his eyes never make contact, always seem to be searching for something just beyond his reach.

But tonight. Carlotta. The red dress. The dim light. The schnapps. He suddenly feels reckless.

"Excuse me," he says, more or less in her direction. The eggnog schnapps makes his stomach tilt and whirl.

Carlotta slowly turns toward him. Her lips are slightly wet, pouty. This frightens Trot. He's promised himself he wasn't going to say anything, but "excuse me" just seems to fall out of his mouth. And now, Carlotta's right eyebrow is raised slightly, expectant. She's waiting for him to say something more, but he seems to have lost the power of speech.

He would like to ask her if she'd like to go fishing sometime, not to catch anything, just to sit in the boat where it's quiet and watch the sunset. He wants to tell her that the sight of the sun setting is beautiful in this part of the world, really something. The sky turns so pink it's pinker than shrimp, or flamingos, or hibiscus, or Pepto-Bismol, or anything else that's so pink it says, "Welcome to Florida" in that two-for-a-buck-postcard sort of way.

It's just pinker than pink ever had a mind to be.

He would like to say all these things, but "Peanuts" is what he says and then points at a bowl in front of her. She's Leon's girl, after all. Everybody knows that.

"Go ahead. They're yours," she says and gently pushes the bowl toward Trot. Her voice reminds him of crushed velvet, of prom night. Makes him sweat.

It's happening again, he thinks, because it is. Ever since high school, ever since Trot and Leon were thin and wiry and Pop-Tart tan and Slam-Book reckless, Leon always gets the girl, even the ones he doesn't want all that much. Trot gets peanuts.

He pops one into his mouth, and Carlotta picks up her cell phone. Punches the keys with her perfect cherry pie nails.

She's probably trying to call Leon, Trot thinks. Leon's probably trying to avoid the call.

"On Christmas Island," Jimmy Buffet sings. "Your dreams come true."

The words make Trot's face go hot.

The phone rings unanswered. Carlotta gets up and wobbles across the room, slaps the jukebox with the flat of her hand. "Don't you have any real music?" she asks no one in particular. "Something with a little kick?" She shakes the sequins of her short red dress like a dog after rain.

Scottish terrier, Trot thinks. Feels an urge to bark.

"I want to dance," Carlotta says and runs a hand through her hair. It pulls it away from her face just for a moment. In the twinkling of red and green Christmas lights, Trot sees she has a scar that stretches down along her hairline. It's thick as lace. He remembers seeing a scar like this once, a long time ago, the aftermath of an explosion at the gas station.

Battery acid, he thinks, and his heart breaks just a little.

"Nobody wants to dance with me?"

Carlotta's voice cracks. People look away. Trot's heart breaks a little more.

Bender leans across the bar, tosses him two quarters for the jukebox. "Go on," he says. "Nice girl like that shouldn't be alone on Christmas Eve."

Trot looks at the quarters, and then at Carlotta. Suddenly, fueled by the type of courage that only eggnog schnapps can provide, he moves across the room. Takes her hand in his. Holds it as if it's made of spun sugar.

"I'm not much of a dancer," he says quietly.

She smiles, lopsided. "Neither am I."

Trot puts the quarters in the jukebox. Presses D12 without looking. When Trot was in high school, D12 was "Black Magic Woman." It's been a long time since high school. "Rudolph the Red Nose Reindeer" falls onto the platter. The needle catches the grooves.

· · ·

Two blocks away, Leon thinks of Carlotta waiting for him and feels a pang of remorse. Then deals from the bottom of the deck. Two aces.

Come on, he thinks, two more aces.

But the cards feel stiff in his hands. Unwilling. Unlucky. Hinky. That's not good.

Leon knows he really should be at The Pink. Knows he shouldn't be playing poker, especially on Christmas Eve. And he knows this, not just because he's lost nearly everything he owns. It's more than that. It's about her. Carlotta. The tunnel of love hips. The way they bump up against you in the dark.

Of course, that's what he says about most women.

Still. He knows he should be at The Pink, but he's not. He's at Lucky's RV Round-Up. It's his place. He owns it.

Won it from Lucky more than ten years ago. There's not much to round up, though. Just a couple used Winnebagos and a transmission from a 1971 Gremlin.

But Lucky's is his. And he's nearly proud of it.

Across Leon's desk, the stranger lays out five diamonds. Ten. Jack. Queen. King. Ace. Leon looks away. He wants to curse, but can't. It's Christmas Eve and he's playing five-card stud with Jesus, or at least some version of him—long brown hair, scraggly beard, sandals, and a white bed sheet wrapped around his bony little waist.

Man, Leon thinks. What kind of a world you got going on inside your head?

The man's skin is so dark he could be Cuban, or Mexican, or just too tan from standing on the side of the road preaching redemption, or whatever crazy Jesus guys do when they're being crazy. Leon can see the man's hands have scars on the tops of them, deep and jagged, like nail wounds. Probably on his feet, too. He wants to ask him how long he's been Jesus. Wants to know if he gets a 10 percent senior discount at the movies because technically, as Jesus, he's older than dirt. But Leon doesn't say a thing. There's something about the man that stops him. He has these odd eyes. It is like this Jesus has some sort of cosmic X-ray vision, like the kind you can buy in the back of X-Man comic books, like the kind you can use to look at girls' underwear.

Like that, but spooky.

Jesus takes the deck and shuffles. The cards fan with peacock precision.

"For a messiah, you sure shuffle like a shark," Leon says and runs a hand though his sandpaper hair. Jesus says nothing. Blows on the top of the deck and taps it twice. A habit he apparently picked up somewhere, Leon thinks, probably not in heaven.

"How about kings are wild?" Jesus asks. "That's been my experience."

Leon wants to laugh, but sees that Jesus is not joking, so he just nods. Man, he thinks, he sure does look like Jesus.

Leon should know. In Florida, Jesus is everywhere. From the "Jesus Is Lord All You Can Eat Buffet" to "Truckin' for Jesus U-Haul." It's as if it's his winter headquarters. Short, tall, male, or female—it doesn't matter—when you least expect it Jesus will be walking barefoot down the center median of the highway, smiling a twisted toothy smile, and waving furiously. Sheet flapping in the wind.

Last year the Florida State Highway Patrol picked up approximately six thousand versions of Jesus. The entire state of Florida is 58,560 square miles, or 37,478,400 acres, including the Everglades, so that would average out to about one Jesus every ten square miles. Give or take a few yards.

That's a lot of Jesus. Leon thinks it has something to do with the heat.

At this moment, however, Leon wishes he'd never seen this one. He was minding his own business when it happened, that's what he plans to tell Carlotta. Just closing up at the Round-Up when Jesus pulls up in the biggest, most expensive recreational vehicle Leon had ever seen.

"We don't have sewer hookup," Leon said and ran a hand over the careful pinstripe of the driver's side. "Nice chrome though; makes you squint."

"I'm just looking for a friendly game of cards," Jesus said. His voice, a dark rumble.

Leon understood. Nodded. The only biblical verse he knows ran through his head—*I saw a stranger and I took him in.* "I can be mighty friendly," he said.

Jesus just smiled. Then he did something odd, something Leon didn't expect. He closed his eyes and leaned across the RV's window and touched Leon on his chest, near his heart. Leon could feel the heat of his hand, feel his own pulse quicken.

"She thinks of you often," Jesus said.

And for whatever reason, Leon knew he was talking about Dagmar, his ex-wife. He doesn't know how he knew, but he knew. And he could feel her cheek brush his lips. Could feel her skin, soft as magnolias. Made his eyes water.

Then he thought of Carlotta and his throat went tight.

About 2 A.M. the stakes turn high. Leon has just put his own motor home on the table and a new pair of eel-skin Acme boots.

Jesus is betting the American Dream.

Chapter 2

The American Dream recreational vehicle is what is affectionately known as a "land yacht." It's forty feet long, has two satellite dishes, two air conditioners, a Zip-Dee awning, and real marble floors in the kitchen. How many miles it gets to the gallon is unimportant. Leon wants it. Needs it. Is determined to get it any way he can. It's his ticket out of Whale Harbor, and he knows it. He can see himself and Carlotta heading down to Miami to sell it and start all over again in a town that has more than one zip code. And no memory. And lots of rum.

But it's dealer's choice and Jesus is dealing. It is his birthday, after all.

"Five-card stud," he says. Places two cards down in front of Leon. "Two down. Two up. The final one down."

"Sure, sure," Leon says.

It's not the normal way to play five-card stud, but the guy thinks he's Jesus, so normal seems to be a relative term.

Outside, the wind presses against the tin walls of the dealership. The fluorescent light above their heads hums, makes Leon's palms sweat. "Sure, sure," he says again for no reason. He just likes the way the word shakes in his mouth. Like dice. Like seven, then eleven. Like snake eyes. The words feel lucky, and Leon knows he needs as much luck as he can get. Jesus is all business for a man wearing a bed sheet—and a shark. Leon knows that for sure. The man never gets excited or raises his voice. Never breaks eye contact. No small talk. He's obviously done this before; cards flow through his bony fingers like creek water, rapids.

Leon looks at his own cards—six of hearts, eight of hearts—he tries hard not to smile. Two hearts beating for Ole Daddy Leon, he thinks. Then Jesus deals him his third, the seven of hearts.

Leon nearly weeps. Three hearts. Three hearts beat as one. A three way. The Holy Trinity of Love.

Then Jesus deals himself the king of spades. Suddenly the room feels two sizes too small.

"Aren't you going to look at your other cards?" Leon asks, tries not to plead. "The ones on the bottom?"

Leon desperately needs him to pick up those cards. Behind Jesus' head there's a mirror. Dusty. Greasy. You can hardly see yourself in it. The word *Airstream* is embossed across it in large silver letters with a tiny toaster of a trailer behind them. But still, if the angle is right, Leon has a perfect view of his opponent's hand. That's why he always plays cards at the dealership. That's why it's still called "Lucky's."

Jesus shakes his head. "More fun this way," he says.

If you're insane, Leon thinks. Which, of course, the man is—and that makes Leon even more frustrated. He wants to reach across the desk and shake this man who looks so much like Jesus that Leon wishes his eighth-grade teacher, Sister Mary Thomas, was there because she'd pee her pants. He wants to shout, "Snap out of it! A guy with your talent belongs in Las Vegas peeling tourists like tangerines!"

But he doesn't, there's too much at stake.

"Okay, then," he says, tries to sound calm. Lifts the corner of his own cards again, just to double-check. Six, seven, eight. All hearts. All his. A possible straight flush, and a straight flush beats all.

His brain hums like a power line. *Come on, baby,* he says to himself as if he's at jai alai again. Leon loves jai alai when he can afford it. The ball leaves the wicket at one hundred miles an hour. His heart pounds patent leather. At jai alai, he's alive and at the top of his game, losing money at a speed faster than he can drive. Anywhere else, he's a pinkie turning green, flaked down to the base metal.

"You in?" Jesus asks and looks at Leon with those Bible eyes.

Shit, Leon thinks. Just can't get a read on this guy. Has no idea what he's holding. But Leon's right hand is itching—and right means money. Three lucky hearts beating as one. "Sure. Sure," he says, and his hand itches even more.

"Then make your bet," Jesus says.

"Sure. Sure."

Outside Lucky's RV Round-Up the neon sign hisses. On the sign there is a cowboy that looks a lot like Leon, but his name is Bob—Bob the Round-Up Cowboy. Leon had the name trademarked. Someone once told him that it would be a good idea. He's still not sure why, but it sounded good at the time. So Leon filled out the forms and sent in the money. A month later, Bob the Round-Up Cowboy was trademarked and legal and all his.

Leon loves that cowboy. Loves the way his hat sits at a rakish angle. Loves his peeling Dennis the Menace eyes. Loves his mystery. Loves the way Bob always seems to be roping something you can't see. The spinning neon lasso shoots out and back again. Snaps and pops.

Sometimes, late at night, Leon stands under the sign and watches it for hours, as if in a dream. From the road, it looks as if the cowboy nearly ropes Leon, but at the last minute the lasso draws back, hissing. Then nearly ropes him again. Then again.

Leon loves the way Bob does that.

But with three hearts beating for Ole Daddy Leon—and an itchy right hand—none of that matters.

"I'll see you the dealership," Leon says.

"*This* dealership?"

Jesus looks around the edges of the dark room. Roaches cover a Diet-Rite can tossed in the corner. A paper napkin tumbles back and forth in slow motion. Other than that, the showroom is empty.

"Just had a big blowout sale," Leon says, and his right hand stops itching. Left one starts.

Damn, he thinks, left is losing.

Jesus is not enthused. He rubs his chin, the bristles of his beard. "I don't know," he sighs. "That's all you have left?"

Leon knows he's in trouble. The American Dream is the Fleetwood Corporation's top of the line. Worth more than a quarter of a million dollars. Lucky's RV Round-Up is a tin shed with windows. A graveyard of parts.

Apparently, this Jesus may be crazy, but not stupid. "Stocks?" he says. "Bonds? Stamp collection? Collectibles? Maybe a set of the sixteen original Hot Wheels circa 1968 still in their original boxes?"

"You've already won everything I have."

"That's sad. Doesn't seem like a lot. Man your age should be more established, don't you think?"

Great, Leon thinks, Sheet-Boy feels sorry for me.

Jesus shrugs. "Well. Okay, then. I guess."

Yes, Leon thinks. Now give me a five.

"Here you go," Jesus says. Deals the five of hearts.

Four hearts beating for Ole Daddy Leon, and his own heart does a tango in 4/4 time.

Then Jesus draws his own card—The king of diamonds. He places it neatly next to the other king. "Two kings," he says in a level voice. "I'll see your Round-Up and raise you life everlasting."

Leon sucks air.

"Raise or fold?" Jesus asks calmly.

Just then Leon's right hand began to itch again. Right means money. Of course, he can see that Jesus has a pair, at the very least, but Leon's right hand is itching and in his mind that means a straight flush is about to fall his way. In his mind, he has Carlotta pinned against the silk sheets in the king-sized bed next to the marble bathroom that he knows is standard in a luxury vehicle like the one parked outside. In his mind, he is a happy man. His thoughts are a ticker tape parade.

Accidentally, his voice slides up three octaves. Pentecostal. "Hit me," he says. "Hit me, Jesus."

"Raise or fold?" Jesus asks again, patiently.

Leon suddenly understands. He blew it. He has to throw something in the pot, or lose it all. But there's nothing left to bet. The sight of all those hearts beating just for him confused him. He upped the ante too fast. His stomach sparks. He feels his pockets for loose change. All he has is two pennies and foil from a gum wrapper.

"Fold?" Jesus asks.

"Hang on."

Leon tosses the coins into the pile. They rattle. He opens his desk drawers. Paper clips. Matches. The ghost of a Bic pen, no ink.

Then he sees it.

"Raise," he says, inspired, and holds up a snack cake, its

cellophane wrapper still intact. Two twin rolls of dark chocolate filled with white icing—and dusty.

Jesus looks at him with what Leon imagines to be a "moneylenders at the temple" kind of frown. "You're betting cake?" he says, incredulous.

Leon feels a bead of sweat roll down his spine.

Sell it, baby. Sell it, he thinks. "It's not just cake," he says and holds it in the palm of his hand like one of those models he's seen on the home shopping channels, "it's devil's food."

The words hiss like a snake looking for a garden, looking for a girl named Eve. I'm going directly to hell, Leon thinks. DO NOT PASS GO. DO NOT COLLECT $200.

"Devil's food?" Jesus says, and his voice quivers. His poker face is gone. He leans across the desk and takes the cake. Sniffs it. His breath is shallow and quick. Leon can see his hands sweat.

Oh, yes. Directly to hell, Leon thinks. "Careful not to squeeze it," he says and lowers his voice reverently as if the cake is made of gold, or titanium, or something actually worth more than three-fourths of a buck.

"Sorry," Jesus says to the cake, not Leon, and puts it down gently in the center of the pile. Can't take his eyes off of it. It's then that Leon notices that across the man's forehead is a series of tiny scars, as if made from a crown of thorns.

Man, Leon thinks, and wants to know why this guy has to be Jesus so badly, who he was before, how he got this way—but doesn't ask. Can't. It would ruin everything. So he says nothing. Tries not to look him in the eye.

"I've never had the devil's food," Jesus says. His mouth is slightly open. His hands tremble with longing.

Leon is nearly pleased with himself. Still got the touch, he thinks, but doesn't feel real happy about it. The scars around Jesus' head look ragged and deep. Must be real messed up to do that to yourself. A horrible feeling of sadness washes over him. What am I doing? This guy is crazy and I'm cheating him. On his birthday.

"Shit," Leon says, "I can't do this." Then he tosses the cake back into the open drawer quickly, before he changes his mind.

Jesus looks panicked. "Can't do what?" His voice is shrill. "Put that cake back."

Leon shakes his head. Closes his desk drawer. He wants to say, it's just a cake. No demonic snack treat. Just lots of preservatives with icing so sweet it will make your cavities cringe. But, before he can say anything, Jesus reaches across the desk and snatches the cake from the open drawer. Tosses it back into the pile of keys and cash.

He's quick for a guy in a sheet, Leon thinks. And angry.

"It's a bet," Jesus says. "Can't change your mind. The cake is in play."

For a moment, Leon considers the absolute truth of the statement and how sweet the truth is, how it can get him off the hook. A bet is, indeed, a bet. Everyone knows that once the stake hits the table, and is accepted, it can never be taken back. It's the rules. It's the truth of the matter. It's the sweet damn truth. And the truth shall set you free.

And besides, Leon tells himself, the cake really is devil's food. It says that on the box. It's not a lie. Just because the snack cake doesn't belong to a fallen angel who is now lingering in eternal hellfire doesn't mean it's not real—but as soon as Leon thinks this, he envisions the nuns of St. Jude's, their saintly faces, their disapproving clucks. Leon always thinks of them in moments of what they would call "spiritual crisis," moments of what he would call "stellar opportunities."

Damn those penguins, Leon shudders, and then accidentally leans back in his chair. It squeaks. Scares the roaches.

"Look," Leon says. "Game over." He picks the cake back out of the pile again. Wipes the dust off it onto his pants. Outside the office window, one of the most expensive luxury coaches in America is winking in the moonlight. Leon's hand stops itching. He feels queasy.

Unfortunately, the crazy guy is not taking no for an answer. He leans across the desk again. His breath is hot. He is angrier than Leon has ever seen anyone be.

"Are you really willing to walk away from this hand? To lose everything you own?"

Leon sputters. He hasn't thought that far. *Everything*, he thinks, is a very big word. "Maybe we can just forget the hand," he says, half-asking, half-pleading.

Jesus laughs and it is not a pretty laugh. It is a howling crazy laugh.

"There's no going back," he says, darkly. "If the cake's not in play, you lose everything you own. Sorry lot that it is."

Jesus picks up the deck and deals the two final cards. One for himself. One for Leon. Both are facedown. "So what will it be?" he says, quietly, seems to know a little bit about temptation himself. "Come on," his voice is reptilian smooth. "You've come this far." He hisses.

The sight of the final card in front of Leon makes his heart beat even faster. He knows he can play through and win, but it just doesn't seem right to cheat a crazy fella on Christmas. If only it was the Fourth of July. Still, "I'm in," is what he says. His legs shake underneath the desk.

Jesus is radiant. He takes the cake from Leon's hand. Places it in the pile again, gently. Pats it. "Okay, then," he says, back to business. "Turn over your card."

Leon hesitates, not so much because he knows the game's not fair—he's already decided that hell can't be much hotter than South Florida in August—but because the guy is right. Crazy, but right. Leon suddenly understands that he's bet his entire sorry pathetic life on this one hand. Well, maybe not his entire life—just his business, his trailer, and his new boots. With a turn of the card, he could be homeless. He could be a man in a sheet with no place to go on his birthday. Could be this guy, he thinks and would like to laugh, but he's never been fond of irony.

And so, for a moment, the two men sit quietly in the ice blue sheen of the fluorescent light. They've been at this nearly all night. Outside, morning begins to push its way through the darkness like a swimmer toward the surface. The corners of the sky are warming. A cat sitting on the chain-link fence squawks like a hungry blue jay but there aren't any birds around yet, just bats with their blindness flying effortlessly and silently back to shelter. Leon puts his hand on top of the final card. He's sweating so badly the card will soon be damp. Even on Christmas he knows he can't get this lucky, especially playing against Jesus. And cheating to boot.

He closes his eyes for a moment. Turns the card over. Can't look.

"Don't be afraid," the man says. "Jesus loves you."

Squeamish, Leon opens his eyes. "Jesus must love me a whole damn lot," he says. The card is, indeed, the nine of hearts. Leon has five hearts beating as one. Five hearts beating for Ole Daddy Leon. At that moment, everything seems to move in slow motion—Leon's brain, his own heart. His mouth is open, gasping. Jesus reaches across the table and makes of the sign of the cross on his forehead, then on his lips. It is a gesture Leon remembers the priests of Ash Wednesday doing long ago. The touch seems to release him.

Then the adrenaline hits.

"I won," Leon screams, then sputters. Tears run down his cheeks. "Thank you Jesus, thank you." He presses his face against the window, looks outside at the American Dream, the tin can beauty of it.

"I can't believe it's mine," he says. His nose is running. "Never had anything this nice before. Women, yes. Plenty of nice women, real good-looking women I had no right fooling with, but I never had anything this nice that doesn't argue with you. You know what I mean? I mean, man. I may just have to buy a new suit just to test drive this thing. Silk tie, maybe. Pink shirt."

Leon wipes his runny nose on his sleeve. "Man, it's so beautiful."

The showroom window fogs from the heat of his breath. He whoops with joy.

"Look at this! Even when you can hardly see it, it's still like the most beautiful thing you'll ever not see!"

Then he turns around. There's no one there. The cards on the desk are laid out in four piles, each pile the same suit. It looks as if he's been playing solitaire, not poker. Everything that Jesus bet is gone. Leon's stomach turns sour. He looks back out at the Dream. It's still there and real enough. The keys are in his hand. The title looks right.

What's the scam? he thinks. Then remembers the moment when he first met Jesus, when he leaned out of the RV's window and placed a hand on Leon's heart.

"She still thinks of you often," he said and now, at this moment, those words make Leon feel so alone, more alone than he's ever felt before.

"Dang, Dagmar," he says. "Even Jesus knows we should still be together. And what does he know about ex-wives?"

The words echo in the empty room.

Chapter 3

Before Ricardo Garcia became Jesus, he'd kept a scrapbook of newspaper clippings. Just bits of information that caught his eye, things he thought he should know.

For example, in Miami, they've cloned Jesus. Raelian leader Claude Vorilhon (aka Rael) was told by an extraterrestrial that he'd encountered on top of a volcano to do so. The extraterrestrial did not leave his name.

In Tampa, they plan to worship Jesus buck naked. When complete, Natura, the first Christianity-themed nudist colony in the country, will be a 240-acre resort area that will have five hundred homes, a hotel, a water-slide park, and a non-denominational Christian church.

In New Smyrna Beach, there's a Jesus Lunch Club at Mom's Diner. If you say your prayers before you eat, you get a 10 percent discount.

Dr. Garcia's scrapbook was filled with things like that, little bits of the world he thought might come in handy some day. Of course, those were the days when he was still a doctor, still answered to "Ricardo Garcia," still identified himself as a second-generation Cuban, although he was vague about his parents.

Back then he had a family practice clinic in the Ybor City neighborhood of Tampa. Coffee-skinned and polite, he was a favorite with all his patients. Gracious in an Old World way. Quiet, which most found reassuring. His practice thrived, though some thought it was odd that he never married. He was, after all, quite a catch.

"Too busy," he told everyone. Besides his practice, he volunteered at the AIDS Hospice two nights a week and would sit with the "rough trade" boys and hold their cold blue-edged hands.

"Do you know Jesus?" he would ask them.

Everyone said that Ricardo Garcia was a good doctor, kindhearted—some said too kindhearted—and thoughtful. Despite his busy schedule, he'd often stop by the homes of his elderly patients, just to check up on them. Ease their pain with a little morphine and a Bible quote. He was known as a religious man, a gold cross Catholic. His only vice was gambling. He seemed to have a sixth sense about cards and could sometimes tell what they were without turning them over. He could never explain how he did this. It was a gift was all he could say.

All in all, Ricardo Garcia thought himself a lucky man—the voices only visited him at night.

But, as is the way with such things, there were eventually, sadly, bodies. That was a problem. So many bodies—each laid out in their Sunday best, their arms crossed, or hands folded in prayer with their eyes sewn shut. Some were eased out of this world with morphine and Bible quotes. Some proved more difficult.

Still, in the end, they were finally at peace. But Dr. Ricardo Garcia wasn't.

And then the forgetting began.

Chapter 4

2 A.M. The Pink is closed and Carlotta, drunk and teary, is off to find Leon.

It isn't a good idea. Trot knows it. Tags along.

"Serve and protect," he explains. "It's my job. Strictly professional." But as they walk together under the rusty moon, Trot finds himself leaning toward her, the warmth of her skin. Carlotta doesn't notice. She's too busy rambling though a list of possible excuses for Leon.

"Heart attack? Amnesia?"

Trot can smell her hair, the green grass perfume of it. "Insanity, maybe. Stupidity. Idiocy—"

"Alligator?"

In Whale Harbor on winter days gators crawl

out of the cold swamp and lie across Main Street like speed bumps. Sun themselves.

"Not likely," Trot says. "Gators just chew on you. They eat cats mostly. Limp birds. Stray dogs."

Mayhem is a subject of particular interest for the sheriff. As he speaks, he picks up speed. "Could've been a panther. That's possible. They'll eat you to the bone. Or a vulture—vultures will pick you apart bit by bit. Shred you like taco meat."

Carlotta's stomach swoops and swirls like a circus daredevil.

"Python," Trot offers, sounds hopeful. "They just squeeze the life out of you, then suck you up like spaghetti."

"There are *pythons* in Florida?"

It is more of a cry than a question.

"Yep. They're not indigenous, though," Trot says, as if this makes a difference. "People just buy 'em, get tired of 'em, and let 'em go. Problem is that they live a real long time. Most people don't know that. So we got generations of them out here."

Carlotta's breath turns shallow. Hands clammy. Heartbeat rapid. Trot continues on.

"I once caught a twenty-two-footer making a snack of a Yorkie, some tourist's dog. One gulp. It was really cool. You could see the bulge of this tiny dog in its belly and hear this little tiny yipping sound—"

It is then that Carlotta squeaks. She wants to scream, but a squeak is all she can manage.

"Yeah," he says, smiling. "Just like that."

She's listening, he thinks. And the mantra begins: I am interesting. I have an interesting job. I am an interesting man.

Trot's mother recently sent him a set of affirmation tapes she received as a bonus during Pledge Week from the PBS station in Miami. She wanted *The Three Tenors,* but unfortunately called at the wrong time.

I am deserving of love.

It is at this moment that Carlotta doubles over.

While it wasn't exactly the reaction Trot was hoping for, he couldn't really say he was surprised.

"You okay?" he asks gently.

Carlotta nods, but isn't okay at all. Schnapps and cream are rising up in her belly like white-water rapids. She starts to gag.

"It's okay," he says and carefully gathers her hair in his hand. It is so soft that it surprises him. He holds it away from her face. Steps back a bit.

"Let her fly, gal," he says softly.

And she does.

When the moment passes Trot takes off his jacket, Sheriff Department issue, and hands it to her. "Wipe your mouth on this," he says. "Everybody does. Department pays for dry cleaning."

Everybody does? Her stomach does a backflip.

"You better now?"

"Not really."

"Hang on. I'll be right back. There's Coca-Cola in the squad," he says and runs down Main Street, back to his car.

Reluctantly, Carlotta wipes her mouth on the nylon shell of his jacket. It smells of gasoline and Brut. She watches Trot running full stride down the street, not jogging. He runs like an athlete. His shoes are polished to a new-car sheen. They glint in the streetlights. Carlotta's never had anyone run for her before. It feels like a heroic and beautiful act, even though he's only going a block.

When Trot arrives at his car, he looks back at Carlotta. She seems so far away. His hand rises up in a wave. Then down again, quickly, as if unsure. But when she waves back, he smiles. Then feels guilty.

Strictly professional, he reminds himself. But runs back even faster.

And of course, as he runs, the warm can of carbonated soda shakes in his hand. Shakes hard.

Carlotta is still smiling when he reaches her. He can feel himself blush, the heat spread over his chest. It makes the tops of his ears turn red. "I always carry a six-pack of cola in the car," he says. "It's warm, but it really settles the stomach."

"You get a lot of people throwing up around here?"

"If you were driving a '72 Mustang without a muffler, you'd be my usual Friday night."

He hands her the can. "Take a swig," he says. "Then spit it out. You'll feel better."

Carlotta tries to open it, but it's difficult. Her nails are long and manicured. Trot watches her struggle for a moment, then takes the can and pops the top for her.

Cola-Cola sprays over them, hissing like a geyser.

"Damn it. Sorry."

Cola drips off his eyebrows and onto his badge. Drips down her face, and down the front of her red sequined dress. Trot tries to brush it off her cheek with the paw of his hand. She looks a little shocked. He shudders. Winces.

Just kill me now, God, he thinks. Get it over with.

But then Carlotta does something unexpected—she laughs. Not at Trot, but at the pleasure of the moment. She laughs at how sweet it is to have someone run for you, to wipe your face, to take care of you, just because. How kind. How amazing.

Her laughter is like wind chimes, uncomplicated in its beauty.

And so Trot laughs, too. At that moment, watching Carlotta standing on the edge of the contents of her stomach, a sense of joy rushes over him. For the first time in a long time, he feels like a happy man. She isn't angry. She understands. He can see that in her face.

"You make me want cotton candy," he says and isn't sure what he means, or if it is the right thing to say, but he feels it, so he says it. Figures she'll somehow understand.

And she does. And stops laughing. She is Leon's girl, after all.

What an idiot I am, Trot thinks.

Carlotta takes the can from his hand. Sips. Spits it out. "Sorry about the jacket," she says quietly and hands it back to him. Takes another sip of the warm soda.

The two walk the rest of the street in silence. But every now and then their bodies knock against each other like bumper cars, give off sparks.

When they finally end up at Lucky's RV Round-Up, the showroom lights are on. They press their faces against the dirty glass of the office window. There, in the fluorescent hum, Leon is sitting across from what seems to be a woman. The long brown hair. The narrow shoulders.

"That SOB," Carlotta says, angry.

That predictable SOB, Trot thinks. Leon's got a new girl. God bless him.

But as soon as Trot thinks this he feels ashamed, feels sorry for Carlotta. She's a nice girl. Probably been through a lot. Deserves better. So he drives her home, even though "home" is Leon's trailer. Trot tries not to think about that too much. The trailer is a 1963 "Sovereign of the Road" Airstream, complete with Sky Dome and extended cab. It shines like a baked potato under the streetlight. Makes Trot's stomach growl.

"Well," she says.

"Well."

"Good night," she says. "Sorry about—"

"No problem. It's my job. Protect and serve, remember?"

"Right."

"Right."

There is nothing else for them to say. And so, in the damp swamp air of Christmas morning with the rusty moon peeling above, Trot and Carlotta stand for a moment, silent. Disheveled. Exhausted. They search each other's faces and see a bit of themselves—the sorrow, the bandaged hearts. So Carlotta leans into Trot. He closes his eyes. She gently kisses his cheek. Takes his breath away.

I am love's catcher's mitt, he thinks sadly.

The touch of her lips burns.

Chapter 5

The Dream Café is not just, as it is still called by the locals of Whale Harbor, a titty bar. Thanks to a new bank loan, they also have a website. Billboards span five miles up and down I-75 to alert drivers on their way to Miami to this fact. Fluorescent green, they feature the high school yearbook photos of Dagmar and the rest of the Pep Squad from St. Jude's class of 1978. Plaid uniforms. Pom-poms. The girls are Clearasil clean and smiling.

"Naughty but Nice!" the caption reads.

The billboards really bring them in.

Underneath the smiling faces fine print, tiny as wayward ants, states that these photos are representative, not the actual photos of women employed at The Dream Café.

Nobody's sued yet, but Dagmar's not planning to go to a high school reunion anytime soon, either.

Dagmar, Leon's ex-wife, is a striking woman. She stands like an Egyptian queen. Honey-skinned, steady brown eyes, apricot hair piled on her head like a Twistee-Freeze. She commands every room she walks into, but never seems to notice. Or care. It's second nature to her.

"The sex we sell here is good clean fun," she tells her dancers. "If we keep it clean enough, we get couples in the door and double our profit."

Since Dagmar inherited the place from her uncle Joe five years ago, there have been a lot of changes. Last year, The Dream Café was identified by *Inc.* magazine as part of the "revolutionary trend in a new user-friendly adult entertainment industry." Wholesome as it profitably can be. There's even tour bus parking.

The Café has always been a family business. Dagmar's mother was a dancer, and Dagmar has worked there for as long as she can remember—first as a bartender, then book-keeper, and then a manager—never danced herself. It only made sense that she would inherit the place. Uncle Joe, a bowling ball of a man, never married.

So, when he died, Dagmar was the only one left. She'd always been interested in business. In between the endless "ons" and "offs" and "on agains" with Leon, she managed to finish a BA in Business Administration at the University of Miami. After graduation, even though she had just had her son, Cal, she planned to find a job with a Miami-based company. Work her way up from the mailroom if she had to.

But Uncle Joe got sick. Then died. And she was stuck. The Dream Café was suddenly hers. The roof leaked. The septic system needed to be replaced. The property taxes hadn't been paid in three years. And Cal was a very colicky baby.

The night after Joe's funeral, Dagmar sat in The Café and tried to come up with a plan—something other than arson. It was Friday and the place was nearly empty except for a foursome of giggling tourists. Dagmar was downwind of them. The air was thick with the scent of coconut oil. They were more or less her age and dressed in a style that is often described in the fashion magazines as "Tropical": expensive, impractical, and carefully designed to scream, "Hey, I'm from Michigan." The men wore pastel cotton sweaters casually tied over the shoulders of their "authentic" Hawaiian print shirts. Collars up, of course. The women had spray-on tans and Lilly Pulitzer sleeveless shifts, just like the ones their mothers wore in the sixties. Slightly corseted. Discreetly zipped up the side. Lemon meringue yellow with tangerine daisies. Bermuda blue with pink flamingos. Tiny bows at the jewel neckline.

They were slumming. Loudly asking if The Café had any champagne without a screw top. Any hollandaise sauce for the french fries? But when the dancers came on stage the foursome grew quiet. Each one bought a lap dance, even the women.

Suddenly, Dagmar understood that sex had a new market share—baby boomers—and a business plan was born.

Now, in the gift shop, vibrators of all sizes are sold shrink-wrapped alongside movies on DVD. Edible panties come in double mocha latte. Body paints in Range Rover green. Uncle Joe would never know the place. Dagmar even tried to get a Starbucks franchise for the lobby, but no luck.

The Café does offer food however, just as it did when Uncle Joe was still alive. It's just like Grandma used to make—except there are naked girls and you don't have to say grace. And the pies are called tarts. And the fish is always sushi grade. And the cheese grits are creatively known as polenta. Instead of Uncle Joe in the kitchen, there are graduates from The School of Culinary Arts in Atlanta. They create reductions with sorghum, mangos, and Chardonnay. Offer goat cheese and guava in phyllo triangles "to start."

The music is the same, though. Five days a week, the blues, the heartbeat of the South, is offered during Happy Hour, courtesy of the Blind Brothers' Blues Band. The band is made up of five elderly black gentlemen. Old school. They are neither blind, nor brothers. Jimmy Ray, the band's front man, has a special place in Dagmar's heart. Always has. Always will. That's why the band is still around, still plays that midnight rough blues.

Jimmy Ray had open-heart surgery a couple of years back. He needs to get to sleep by 9 P.M. Doctor's orders. That's why he and the rest of the fellows play only during Happy Hour now. Dagmar picks him up every night and takes him home, too. She is careful of his dignity. He is an elegant man. Caramel-skinned, handsome, and soft-spoken. Part of the aristocracy of the blues, he claims to have been born on Beale Street, right on the sidewalk. Says his mama went into labor singing for loose change.

It's easy to believe. Jimmy Ray embraces the blues as a birthright with an unsurpassed regal air. Pin-striped suits. Manicured hands. His blue-black hair, now gone silver, is always set in the perfect marcel waves. His skin has that acid old man smell, and he shakes a little, but he still knows how to play the blues and riffs about the life he had, and misses, all smoke and whiskey and big-lipped women reckless as Saturday night. He growls like thunder. Gives you chills.

Forty years ago, when Uncle Joe first hired Jimmy Ray and his band, The Café was well known not only for its dancers, but also for its after-hours club, a "Black and Tan," as such clubs were called.

After all the other bars closed—the bars for "Whites Only," and those where "Coloreds" were allowed to sit near the toilets, but not to use them—anybody who could still drive would cruise over to The Dream Café. Jimmy Ray and the band would play until the sun rose. BYOB. Mixes available. Anything that happened behind The Café's doors stayed there.

At sunrise, the band, the dancers, the drunks, and the lovers—the "black" and "tan" who only had this place, this moment—would all eat breakfast together. It was served family style in overflowing plates passed around the table. Country ham baked in milk with crackling bread and wild orange jelly. Pancakes with cane syrup. And lots of Cuban coffee, sweet and thick.

Growing up, Dagmar and her mother lived in a trailer behind The Café. On Saturday mornings, Dagmar would take her place at the table and have breakfast with the adults.

It was magical. They spoke to her about things she knew nothing about, like politics and travel. It was like being in a movie. The women were birthday cake beautiful with their bouffant hair, pale pink lips, and rhinestones, lots of rhinestones in their ears, on their shoes, sewn into the fabric of their Sunday-best dresses. They sparkled like so many candles. And the men that encircled them, arms casual across the backs of their chairs, Dagmar remembers them, too. Their slick hair, their silk shirts, their diamond rings, and the smell of spice and tobacco. They reminded her of pirates.

She still remembers every detail of those mornings. The way the dawn smelled, the heady mix of salt air and dew. The way people spoke in whispers. But most of all she remembers her mama, Annie. Her hair was the color of peaches, just like Dagmar's, as was her skin. The lack of sleep always made her voice smoky. "Give us a kiss, sugar," she'd growl and pull Dagmar into her tired arms, give her a little squeeze. "You okay, darling?"

And Dagmar would nod, even if she wasn't okay, and hold her mother's face in her small hands like one does a firefly—amazed at the light, not wanting to let go, but knowing you had to.

Her mother had always talked about leaving, about going to a real town like Chicago: a town with something to do, something other than watch each other grow old and die. "Florida is heaven's waiting room," she'd say. "And God's not ready for the likes of us yet."

Sometimes Dagmar would come home from school and find her mother passed out on the couch, smelling of strawberry wine and cigarettes. *General Hospital* blaring on the television. Jimmy Ray would usually stop by around suppertime and bring dinner.

"Mama needs her rest," he'd say, and he and Dagmar would sit on the steps of the trailer and gnaw at the bones of BBQ, or fried chicken.

"We're going caveman today, gal."

And they'd talk about anything and everything, except Annie.

The last time she saw her mother was at Saturday breakfast. Dagmar was just fourteen years old but knew there was something wrong. Annie seemed nervous. Wouldn't look her in the eye. Kissed her too hard. And when the coffee was being poured, she stood up and said, "My baby's learning French." Which was true, but everybody stopped talking and stared. Breakfast wasn't a situation usually given to announcements and her mother's voice was pulled taut.

"That's my girl," Annie creaked. "Citizen of the world." Her eyes were filled with tears.

Most at the table just nodded and went back to their conversations. But Jimmy Ray leaned over to Dagmar and said, "You know, I know some French. Learned in New Orleans. That's a town where they know how to *vo-lay-vo*." And then he winked.

Everyone laughed, but not her mother. Annie leaned into Jimmy Ray and spoke, fierce and low.

"You better keep your *vo-lay-vo* to your *vo-lay* self."

The table went silent. Uncle Joe cleared his throat. Dagmar turned red. Jimmy Ray looked hurt.

"Don't mean no harm, sweetheart," he said to Annie. His voice was whiskey soft. "You know that, no harm at all. I'd kill the man who touched her."

And then Jimmy Ray and her mother exchanged a look that Dagmar would never forget. It was the kind of look she'd seen other men and women give each other. The kind of look that says they have secrets. That surprised her. Until that moment, Dagmar never thought much about Jimmy Ray. He was just there, always, a part of her life. He was like the sun in the morning, like the gators in the creek. She never noticed how he always sat next to her mother. How it was his arm draped over her chair.

She never noticed any of that until they exchanged that look—and then Dagmar noticed everything.

Her mother's eyes narrowed. "You'd better watch over her," she said, roughly. "Better do the right thing."

"The child knows I love her," Jimmy Ray said.

And Dagmar did. Still does. Doesn't need to know much more. The look between Jimmy Ray and her mother said it all. And Jimmy Ray's love, constant and unflinching, confirms it.

Dagmar never saw her mother again. There were plenty of letters postmarked from all over the country, but never Chicago. They all ended with "See you soon. Luv 'Mama," which always struck Dagmar as odd. Annie never liked to be called "Mama." There was never a return address.

When Dagmar turned eighteen, her mother sent her a birthday card with lace edges and a poem about a mother's love. She didn't write "See you soon." She signed it "Ann," not "Mama." Underneath her name was a single sentence: "Being a mama isn't for everybody, but that don't mean I never loved you."

But she never came back.

All Jimmy Ray could say was, "Your mama had a hole in her that love couldn't plug."

And Dagmar inherited it.

All these years later, the heartbroken girl inside of her still waits for her mother's return. That's why she's put her face on the billboards. That's part of the reason she stays. If she left, her mother wouldn't know where to find her. Besides, where would she go? Like it or not, The Dream Café is her home.

"Come join the fun!' it says on the back of the matchbooks. And fun is what Dagmar feels she sells. Twenty-four hours a day. Seven days a week. Three hundred sixty-five days a year. "We are the Wal-Mart of fun," she tells anyone who'll listen, and nearly believes herself, even though it's clear by the look on her face that it's difficult for her to watch the dancers at work, difficult for her to see the calloused hands of the men who sit up close.

"She's got no stomach for it," the dancers say among themselves. Some say it with pity because they know that she'll eventually close the place and that would be a shame.

In towns like Whale Harbor jobs are scarce. You do what you can. What there's a market for. What's more or less legal.

There's a club near Orlando that does Shakespeare in the nude because the town has an ordinance that says that nudity is legal in legitimate theater. "To be or not to be," never had so many layers of meaning before.

But that's the way it is in Florida. It's paradise. The visitors want fun. That's what they pay for. They're gonna have fun if it kills them. Or you. Or both.

So it's 6 A.M. on Christmas morning and The Dream Café is open for business, but it doesn't seem that there's much fun to be had. A handful of truck drivers sit at the edge of the stage. They're not regulars, but Dagmar's seen them once or twice before. They're having breakfast, on the house. Biscuits and gravy. No fancy name for it. Plenty of black coffee served Cuban style, sweet and thick—just like Uncle Joe would have done.

Free breakfast on Christmas is a tradition at The Dream Café that goes back to the Black and Tan days.

"Merry Christmas," Dagmar says as she serves each man personally. Some say "Merry Christmas" back. Some just nod. Some don't say anything, just seem embarrassed. That's understandable. In her white apron, with her apricot hair pulled high on top of her head, Dagmar looks a lot like someone's mother. And behind her, onstage, there's a nearly naked woman writhing.

It is a little unsettling.

But Dagmar doesn't notice. She's just trying to get this over with, serve some damn Christmas cheer, and get out as quickly as she can. Uncle Joe made her promise that she would keep up the tradition and she hates it with a passion. "These guys should be home with their wives and kids on Christmas," she told him.

"That's not for us to judge," he said. "They put food on our table. To return the favor one day a year is the least we can do. To give back is a gift unto itself."

And even though she wanted to tell him that giving food away to moochers who spend their money paying women to get naked and say nasty things to them is perhaps not as blessed an act as Mother Teresa washing the feet of lepers in Africa, she just nodded. Said nothing. And so now she's stuck. It was, after all, a promise. A deal's a deal.

So she tries to concentrate on what Jimmy Ray always tells her. "Look at everyone as Buddha would," he says. "Look with an open heart. Find the goodness within them."

Jimmy Ray is a Buddhist. It's a recent turn of events. The day after he had open-heart surgery he announced it. Just like that. Baptist now Buddhist. Claimed that while he was under anesthetic, he had a vision. Phil Jackson, then coach of the Los Angeles Lakers, and a Buddhist himself, appeared to Jimmy Ray and imparted two revelations that he still holds dear.

The first: "Heaven is a place within your heart."

The second: "Michael Jordan is shorter than you think."

Then Jackson drove off on his Harley-Davidson.

The vision had a profound effect on Jimmy Ray. Now, he tries his best to convert others to the Noble Eightfold Path, the teachings of Siddhartha, The Enlightened One.

"You must approach these men with the Right Understanding, honey," he told Dagmar. "See who they really are without imposing your preconceived notions.

"In other words," he said, "it's all good."

So, when Dagmar serves each man his breakfast, she looks into his eyes and tries to see who's really inside there. She looks for the spark of a divine spirit and prays that there won't be a repeat of last Christmas, when some drunk grabbed a dancer's breast and Dagmar suddenly began to rail on him with a plastic Santa. Then she pushed him into the eight tiny reindeer and they all fell like bowling pins onto the Christmas tree sending glass bulbs skidding across the floor. The bubble lights popped and snapped. The power flickered. Icicles were everywhere. The man began to cry.

The dancers refer to it as "The Christmas Day Massacre."

Luckily, this year, Santa is still standing and her shift is almost over.

"Merry Christmas," she says to the last man at the table. The man, burly, with a head shaved clean as an egg, takes the food hesitantly.

"I don't believe in Christmas, Mrs. I'm sorry." His voice is coarse.

"It doesn't matter," Dagmar says. "Enjoy. There's more if you need it."

She turns to walk away, but he catches her arm. His eyes are steady and cold. "Don't seem right, Mrs. You giving me something in the spirit of something I don't even believe in. And I don't have anything to give you."

The man makes Dagmar uneasy. He is large and broad like a wrestler, a diamond stud in his nose. Despite the cool morning, fifty-one degrees and overcast, he's wearing a leather vest, no shirt. Across his neck is tattooed the word *Grace.*

"That's okay," she says. Her arm is going numb. Dagmar searches his eyes for the divine spirit within him, but finds it's a little tough to get a bead on it without feeling in her fingers.

The man pulls her closer. "Well, if you won't take money, let me give you something else."

The words make her twitch.

She wonders if she starts meditating, *om-mani-padme-hum,* maybe she can find a way out of this situation that would be The Noble Path and would enlighten her and all around her. And, most important, that would help her avoid wildly beating this overgrown monkey with that plastic Santa that seems to be standing, once again, too close at hand.

The others at the table stop talking and watch Dagmar and the man. The rock and roll blares on. ZZ Top is singing the titty girl standard, "She's got legs. She knows how to use them."

Dagmar really hates that song. Onstage, Bernie is dancing. She's older than the rest but enthusiastic and cheerful. Has a solid following with couples. The green tassels of her pasties spin like propellers, but no one seems to notice. The man pulls Dagmar even closer. She feels his stale breath against her arm. Up close, he looks older than she first thought—somewhere in his fifties. Steroid strong.

"Give me my arm," she says, the stern mother. "Or I'll kick your ass from here to Tallahassee."

It isn't Buddha's way, but it works. The man lets her go.

"Sorry," he says. "I just get insistent sometimes."

"That's okay." She straightens her apron. Adjusts the tower of her hair.

He clears his throat, "You see, people sing for their supper. That's what I meant."

Dagmar isn't quite sure she heard him right. "You want to sing?"

"Not exactly," he says. "It's not a song. It's a prayer I learned in Vietnam during the war. We took some priests captive at a shrine—"

He trails off for a moment and the dark look on his face fills in the details. Gives Dagmar a chill.

"Anyway," he says, "they sing this at sunrise. It's just about sunrise, isn't it?"

Dagmar nods. The ZZ Top song is blessedly over. Bernie stands at the edge of the stage, adjusting her G-string. The man clears his throat, closes his eyes. His voice is hopeful. Fragile. Eerie.

"Chuẻ̀ng con caàu xin nhôo Chuùa Kitoâ, Thieân Chuùa vaø Ñaáng Cöùu Chuoäc chuẻ̀ng con."

The words are as fragile as old bones. When he finishes, he bows his head as a sign of respect.

"That's beautiful," Dagmar says. "What does it mean?"

"Whatever you need it to."

A few of the men nod in agreement. One of them says, "That's why we call him the Preacher. He's always talking deep shit."

"That's nice," Bernie says and touches him gently on the shoulder. "Thanks."

Preacher blushes. His fellow drivers look surprised.

"Hey, I got something I can trade for food," another man says. "Something that will make you laugh 'til you weep."

Out of his greasy blue jean jacket he pulls a picture of his wife and their new baby. The drooling child is stuffed into a Christmas stocking. He looks a lot like a beefsteak tomato. His red face is cocked to one side. A tiny green bow is glued to his head. He is cross-eyed.

Dagmar does, indeed, laugh.

"Ugly, isn't he?" the father says proudly. "Takes after his old man."

"How old?"

"Six weeks too early. Finally gets out of the hospital today. I got to eat and run. Damn. Working on Christmas is a damn bitch."

And that's when it hit her. They're working, Dagmar thinks. They'd rather be home with their families. She suddenly feels her Buddha heart open to him, and Preacher, and all the rest. She suddenly feels a fleeting moment of happiness to be on The Noble Path—with the plastic Santa and his tiny reindeers all still standing.

"It's all good," she says with a Pep Squad lilt.

The men look at her oddly. Apparently not Buddhists, she thinks.

"Baby's okay now?" Dagmar asks. "I know they can do a lot for preemies these days."

The father shrugs. "He's doing. That's what we say. Doing one day at a time."

Onstage, Bernie is tired. Her hair, which is dyed an un-natural shade of red, now sticks up straight in several places. Makes her look like the flame of a match. It's been a long night. Her elf suit and elfin cap are scattered at her feet, the remnants of a holiday tribute. Her green pasties, no longer in motion, wilt.

"Anybody want to talk dirty? I can be a bad, bad girl," she says.

The men shake their heads.

"Know any Christmas carols?" Preacher asks. "I feel I can use some more singing."

In her ten years as a dancer, Bernie can safely say she's never has a request for Christmas carols before. She looks at Dagmar for guidance.

"Up to you," Dagmar says.

Bernie grins. "Well, shoot. I'm a good Catholic girl," she says. "I know more Christmas carols than the pope, but I don't want to sing alone."

"I don't sing good, but I'll sing," says the driver with the photo of his baby. "Gots to practice for the kid."

"Sure," another says. "We'll all sing."

"Okay, then," Bernie says. She walks to the middle of the stage, a stage on which earlier she did things with cola bottles that made them nonrefundable in several states. She suddenly looks shy and gangly, awkward as a girl.

"Go ahead," Dagmar says. "Just pick a song and we'll all join in."

The truck drivers put their forks down. Some clap. Some take a sip of coffee. Preacher clears his throat. Bernie adjusts her thong again and smooths the tassels of her wilted pasties. When she finally finds her courage and begins to sing, her voice is pure and sweet. The type of voice one associates with angels.

"Oh come all ye faithful. Joyful and triumphant."

The men, one by one, join in. Their voices shake a bit. Some go flat. Dagmar looks at their faces, softened by the moment, and can, indeed, see their Buddha hearts. Unpolished, yet luminescent.

She would like to sing along, but finds she can't. She's crying. She's not sure why.

That's okay, she tells herself. She has to go to Jimmy Ray's. He'll be waiting. Can't be late.

She grabs the elf's cap from the stage and puts it on. Nods good-bye, but nobody notices. Bernie and the men just keep on singing. Each is naked in his way. Each wounded. Each blessed. Their awkward voices are raised together in song honoring a boy who wasn't born too early like the truck driver's baby, but died too soon.

Dagmar knows a lot about babies that die too soon. Too much, she thinks, and pushes away the memory of Cal, her own son. This is her first Christmas without him.

When she gets into her car, the old Mercedes convertible her uncle Joe left to her, she puts the top down. The cold air feels good against her face, wakes her up a bit. But she can't stop crying. Her caffeine heart speeds.

When she finally turns onto the dirt road that used to be paved, used to have a sign that welcomed visitors to Whale Harbor, she is going too fast. Nearly loses her elfin cap. Gravel chews her tires. Christmas presents tumble like dice. Up ahead, she can see the trademarked Bob the

Round-Up Cowboy and his lasso aimlessly spinning in the air—coming up short, coming up short again—and, surprisingly, what appears to be Jesus walking in the center of the road toward her.

At first she thinks it's a hallucination. But as she drives past, he waves a bony hand. It catches her attention and the eerie delicate prayer of Preacher's song came back to her.

Buddha heart, she thinks. Never know where you find one.

She slams on the brakes. The car fishtails. She idles for a moment.

Dagmar has never picked up a hitchhiker before. She looks at the man in the rearview mirror. He is slight of build, and too thin. Doesn't seem armed, just lost. Maybe he's on the way to a church pageant, she thinks. Backs up slowly. Have a little faith, she tells herself but her heart beats even faster.

"Need a ride?"

The man leans into the car. Looks at her closely. His sheet billows in the cold morning air. For some odd reason he smells like devil's food cake.

"You must be Dagmar," he says and smiles.

"Happy Birthday," she says, without thinking.

Chapter 6

Leon stands in his stocking feet, eel-skin boots in hand, and stares for a moment at the American Dream. The keys make his hand itch. It's Christmas morning, just past six. Leon wants to call Carlotta but figures she's turned her cell phone off, so he doesn't bother. Figures he'll deal with it later.

The chrome of the Dream shimmers in the sunrise. Leon shimmers, too.

Carlotta, however, is not currently inclined to shimmer. She is hungover and seasick in Leon's custom waterbed. In her dreams, she is screaming at him with hurricane force. The words hit at 100, 110 miles per hour, roar around Leon, ripping off his shirt, making his hair stand on end. He's wet and cringing. Toasters, TVs, Castro Convertible sofa beds fly through the air at him, nearly missing, but she just keeps on screaming. In the corner of her dream a meteorologist with Super Doppler Radar is tracking her in a live shot. The world spins around the weatherman in his perfect trench coat, his TV tan, and bleach bright teeth. His hair doesn't move. Carlotta likes that.

"That's the kind of man I want," she thinks, still sleeping. Rolls over.

· · ·

Leon is in trouble and he knows it. Can sense it. Knows he should go home and see Carlotta. Leave right now, and, on the way, stop at the 7-Eleven and buy a gallon of Rocky Road just to help smooth things over. And a fashion magazine. Maybe some piña colada air fresheners. A silk rose. Mars bars—bags of them. At this point, he knows it's going to take a lot of stuff to make Carlotta happy again, more than just the usual beef jerky and unsalted pumpkin seeds. Besides standing her up last night, Leon has also forgotten to buy a Christmas gift. Once the Rocky Road is gone, Carlotta is sure to notice. He knows that. Even the American Dream can't change that fact.

But, instead of climbing into his mandarin orange 1975 El Dorado—a ragtop complete with matching citrus-toned leather and whitewall tires, a "Pimp Daddy Caddy" that could be a collector's item if it wasn't nearly rusted through—Leon walks over to the Dream. He walks in his stocking feet, boots in hand, carefully, gently, slowly over the broken clamshell driveway, over the frozen burrs that cross-hatch the weeds. Doesn't even want to take the time to put his shoes on. Just wants to look inside. He's never owned anything this beautiful before. Just one look before he goes. That's all he wants. One look can't hurt anything.

"You sure are nice," he says under his breath. "You sure are pretty."

One quick look. Then over to the 7-Eleven. Then home.

In the distance, there's the sound of eighteen-wheelers on U.S. 41, roaring like the ocean. You can also hear the faint bark of a dog, the dog that always seems to bark in the slow hours of morning. And, if you listen closely, you can also hear the grinding whine of Dagmar's Mercedes as she downshifts from 90 mph to stop to ask Jesus if he wants a ride.

But Leon doesn't hear any of it. He unlocks the driver's door and feels his future unroll in front of him like a red carpet on the corner of Hollywood and Vine. He takes his wraparound sunglasses from his shirt pocket and puts them on, just because. The door handle is cool to the touch. Inside the American Dream there are real leather chairs, instead of bucket seats. Leon brushes off the bottom of his pants and sits down softly. Wishes he'd had a bath.

He closes the door slowly. It moves so easily in his hand, he can hardly believe it. Doesn't snap and crack on its hinges like the door in his mandarin orange El Dorado. It just shuts calmly with a whoosh, then a loud click. Startled,

Leon jumps then looks around to see if anyone saw. A jackrabbit runs across the parking lot. Leon takes a deep breath. Automatic locks. Man, that's nice, he thinks. Opens the door again quickly, just to be sure he isn't locked in. Then shuts it. Doesn't want to let any of the new car smell escape.

As the sun rises higher in the sky, Leon leans over and takes a huge whiff of the passenger's seat. His sunglasses slip off his nose onto the sweet cream leather. It doesn't matter. The moment is perfect. A feeling of well-being settles over him.

He is unaware that, right now, at home, in his own RV, Carlotta had fallen out of the waterbed and is now as awake as a rabid dog—and as industrious. His only suit is being heaved across the gravel yard of the motor court and is tumbling toward the swamp. His beer can collection now rocks back and forth in the gentle morning breeze, wrinkled like so many accordions. Clyde, the six-foot stuffed brown bear Leon won the week before from the taxidermist in Florida City, looks on in stuffed horror. But at this moment, Leon thinks of nothing but the new leather air of the American Dream. Tears fill his eyes.

Gently, he turns the key in the ignition, the engine kicks to life. Then hums. Leon wipes the tears from his face with his sleeve. The air is electric with dings and buzzers. The dashboard looks like a cockpit. LED lights flicker, turn his face blue. Leon wants to take the Dream for a spin, but it's not like anything he's ever driven before. There are no rearview mirrors; just two video cameras connected to a twenty-inch flat-screen TV that's built into the dashboard between the driver and passenger's chairs. He touches the screen. There's a spark. Static electricity.

"Sorry," he says.

On the dashboard, there's a small computer screen about the size of a hand. "The Global Position Satellite" is printed in neat silver letters. Leon presses the "On" button. Deep in space, a satellite flying over New Jersey latches on to his signal. As does another near the Bermuda Triangle. As does a third that is slipping across the sky of Orlando over the sleeping Magic Kingdom. The signals converge. A tiny map appears on the screen with an "x." "You are here." The "x" floats outside of U.S. 41; looks as though no roads connect him with the interstate to Miami. He types in the words *Miami Beach, FL.* The screen states that Miami is approximately 89.7 miles, 105 minutes away. One hundred and five minutes until he can order an ice cold Busch, poolside, surrounded by widows with faces tight as Saran Wrap. That is, if he leaves now. In half an hour, somewhere around 7 A.M., the tourists will wake up—then it will be four hours or more, if he's lucky.

Leon looks at the gas gauge. Nearly empty. If he runs out of gas, he knows he'll need a wrecker to get the Dream down to the freeway to the nearest gas station. Nobody in Whale Harbor is open on Christmas Day. The American Dream gets about eight miles to the gallon; you can't just fill up a bunch of those red cans and hope for a headwind. But, for just a brief moment, he's willing to try.

He sighs and turns off the computer. The satellites lose sight of the Dream once more.

"Bye. Bye," he says. Takes off his socks. Doesn't want to

make the floors dirty. He walks carefully across the honey-colored marble. "Man. Oh, man." The floor is cold, but it's a rich cold, he thinks. A better grade of cold.

The American Dream is like no other recreation vehicle he's ever seen. Not up close, at least. Looks like it rolled off the pages of a magazine. Behind the driver's seat there's a leather couch. Ivory. Beyond that, a galley kitchen with a microwave, convection oven, and dishwasher. Leon opens up a kitchen cabinet. Inside are china cups with tiny straw-berries painted on them. The strawberries are small and sweet, just like the ones he used to watch the migrant workers pick from the fields outside of town. The cups are delicate, tiny handles. Carefully, he picks one up, sticks out his pinky. This is living.

But when Leon opens the door to the small refrigerator, he thinks again of Jesus. Imagines him alone, walking somewhere down the highway. The refrigerated air makes him feel even colder.

How could a Jesus guy get a thing like this? And why would he want to get rid of it?

Winning was just too easy. Leon suspects Jesus was counting cards, setting him up. But why? It doesn't make sense. Most guys try to win a rig like this, not lose one. First thing on Monday, Leon knows he needs to run a check on the title through the DMV. That would be the smart thing to do, and that's exactly why he's not going to do it.

"Ignorance is bliss."

That's the one bit of advice Lucky gave him about the

used RV business. It's the only firm and fast rule, he told him. "It's like our code of honor."

And Leon's stuck by it. Plans to hold fast to a blissful state of ignorance as long as he owns the Round-Up. Everybody's got to have a moral code, he thinks and pops a perfect ice cube into his mouth and feels exhausted, overwhelmed by good fortune. All he wants to do is close his eyes for a minute. Ten-minute nap, and then off to the 7-Eleven, then home.

He walks past the tile steam shower with two massage heads, the matching pearl-tone toilet and bidet, and into the bedroom to the king-sized bed. The walls are real oak. On top of the silk bedspread there's a dozen tiny pillows, lace-edged and mouse-sized.

He brushes off his pants again and sinks into the soft bedspread. The mattress is a little lumpy, which surprises him, but the moment is silk and sleep. The sheets have a blue smell, like dry-cleaned flowers. Leon rolls back and forth in them.

Better than love, he thinks. But I have to sell it. Maybe that's the catch. I can have it because I can't have it. But I'll itch for it, like Dagmar.

As sleep wraps around him, Leon thinks he hears the coo of his mama's voice. He startles awake, coughing. Sees himself in the bathroom mirror. Mama Po's been gone a long time, ten years, give or take a few days. And Cal, his son, only a year.

"It's all right," he says to his reflection. His eyes are red rimmed. "It's okay, man." Then he lies back down on the bed, covers each eye with a tiny lace pillow. The pillows smell like lavender. It's okay, he tells himself. It's okay.

But it isn't.

There's a very good reason why the mattress is not as comfortable as one would expect a brand-new Posture-Perfect to be. Duct-taped along the bottom of the bed is a large plastic bag filled with $100s—$350,000 in $100s, to be exact. Ira and Rose Levi had grown up in the Depression and didn't trust banks completely. No wire transfers for them. When it was time to move from Cicero to Miami, Rose taped their nest egg to the bottom of the bed so no one would find it.

And no one did. Of course, now it doesn't really matter. The Levis won't need it anymore.

But Leon doesn't know this. All he knows is that he's tired. So he tries to fall asleep and dream of Mama Po and the old days when he was a boy, like Cal. Tries to dream of the magic of Whale Harbor; tries to dream of a time when his life was simple and good and he was happy.

But it's a little difficult. His right hand itches as if on fire. Right means "money."

Chapter 7

When Leon was a boy, Whale Harbor used to be a town devoted to fun. Used to be the streets smelled of blue snow cones. The sun shone caramel corn. Buddy's Snake Petting Zoo sat next to the Whale Harbor Municipal Go-Cart Park, and the famed Ishmael & Son's Whale Watching Charters. The town had its own Ferris wheel. The merry-go-round was open year-round.

Back then Pettit's All-Star Alligator Farm was the main attraction. Leon's grandmother, Lettie Pettit, opened the place in 1960, right after Hurricane Donna. Operating a tourist attraction was never what the steel-spined woman had in mind, but she would later say it was divine destiny. And on some level she was entirely right.

Donna was the worst hurricane Florida had ever seen. Its eye was twenty-one miles wide. Winds sustained at 180 mph, gusts clocked in at 200.

"Sounded like the hooves of a thousand horses," Lettie later said. "Like the horses of Armageddon."

Hurricane Donna changed everything for most in this small town. Seventy-five were killed. The oyster beds were ruined. Houses were tossed like dice.

And Pettit's All-Star Alligator Farm was born.

Lettie had no choice. Her house had completely vanished; a sinkhole swallowed it whole. There was just a small deep lake where the pink clapboard used to be.

When she saw the destruction, she stared at the murky water, the thin layer of green algae, and the occasional bubble that rose from it, and said nothing. The only thing that remained of what was once her home was a rambling white fence and its gate that nearly shut tight.

When she finally spoke, "God's will," she said, and the words sounded more like a cough, rough and low. It was clear that everything was lost except for the Pontiac she and her daughter, Po, drove to the shelter with.

"At least we got some place to sleep," Po said quietly. She was just seventeen years old and eight months pregnant. The father was long gone. She looked on the verge of tears.

"This sorrow is not part of our bones," Lettie told her daughter. "It's just looking for a place to rest a while."

And then Lettie, who was an oysterman's widow from a long line of oystermen's widows, did the only thing she could do, a thing she did well—she made do.

She and Po drove into the next town and bought five pounds of chicken necks and fishing line. Then, armed with the necks and fast footwork, the women lured more than a dozen gators from a nearby creek into the sinkhole that was once their house. Slammed the gate behind each one. Tied it tight.

Once the alligators, or "All-Stars" as Lettie had begun to call them, were rounded up she bought two hammers, a truckload of lumber, a case of varnish, fourteen sacks of flour, six gallons of green paint and one of red. Two straw hats to ward off sunstroke. Lettie had a plan.

"And a plan," she told Po, "is more than most people have."

Even though she had no idea of how to create a top-rate tourist attraction, Lettie knew one thing for sure—it needed an entrance gate that could not be forgotten, something that grabbed attention and created a sense of wonder and excitement. So, using the All-Stars as models, the Pettit women fashioned themselves a twelve-foot-high alligator head, complete with an assortment of pointy teeth and a long red tongue. Varnished it until it was rock hard.

It was, certainly, an entrance gate like no other. Leaned a little to the right.

"That sure do look pretty," Po said and tried to mean it.

Over the alligator's huge gaping mouth a sign read, "You pays your money, you takes your chances."

And the tourist attraction was born. Three days later, so was Leon.

And so, for many years, a steady stream of visitors lined up two deep and walked into the gigantic gator grin to see Pettit's All-Stars. The alligators themselves were huge and hungry behind the peeling fence. "Quite a sight," proclaimed the one-line listing in Florida's official tour book. And it was. Every now and then something from Lettie's sunken house would make its way to the surface—a wedding photo or Po's old teddy bear—and the gators would rush toward it roaring and focused. Visitors would "ooh" and "ah."

But the star attraction of Pettit's was Miss Pearl, "The Amazing One-Ton Wonder." Pearl was toothless and too lazy to be mean. Older than anyone could remember. When Lettie saw the docile alligator, she tied a straw hat around its head. The hat had a band of pink daisies, the price tag still hanging from it.

"She looks just like Minnie Pearl," Lettie laughed.

"You sure are a looker, Miss Pearl," Po said and itched her scaly chin as if she were an old fat tabby, Moon Pie–eyed, and low to the ground.

Miss Pearl just yawned.

After that, four times a day, at 10 A.M., noon, 2 and 4 P.M., Po, in a cheesecake-tight swimsuit, leaned over the fence and shook a whole chicken in front of Miss Pearl's gigantic face. "What you say, Miss Pearl?" she'd ask. "Can you say 'howdy'?"

The other alligators seemed to look away in shame as Po would shake the chicken hard and the plucked bird would shimmy from left to right as if doing the Peppermint Twist. "Let's hear a 'howdy' for the good ole folks, Miss Pearl," Po would say, praline sweet.

And, four times a day, the enormous alligator who had never been to the Grand Ole Opry would rub up against Po like a fat spoiled cat and wail an unearthly high pitched wail. It was a wail that sometimes, under the unrelenting subtropical sun, sounded like the Nashville star, but most days just sounded as if the alligator had a one-ton case of indigestion from swallowing all those chickens without chewing first.

"Amazing, isn't it?" Po would ask the crowd, then smile. Back then Mama Po was an angel in Spandex: creamy-skinned and Esther Williams slim. No matter what she'd say, all the men would clap. The women, reluctant and slightly green-eyed with envy, would nod and cluck.

But when the new highway was finished, visitors didn't have to drive near Whale Harbor anymore. Didn't come to whale watch. The Ferris wheel rusted in place. Vandals took apart the merry-go-round, bit by bit, chewing away at it like field mice. At the zoo, the snakes just slipped away.

Lettie died that season. Leon was only twelve years old when it happened. He was teetering in that limbo between childhood and manhood. His body, an odd giant. He came home from school one day and found Lettie in the ticket booth, her blue eyes, skyless. Her hand was still holding a ticket, waiting for the visitors who never seemed to come anymore. Lettie had been dead for hours. Nobody noticed except for the flies.

After that, Po and Leon often went hungry, feeding the gators instead of themselves. "Them snowbirds will be back," Po said. "Nobody can forget Miss Pearl."

After two winters, it became obvious that the visitors weren't coming back to Whale Harbor. Not now. Not ever. Po applied for food stamps. The All-Stars were scheduled to be skinned, sold for shoes. Leon tried hard not to cry.

"Got to be done, baby," Po said and ran a hand through his sun-bleached hair, kissed his cheek, and said nothing more.

The night before the All-Stars were taken away, Leon sat up with Miss Pearl, feeding her a last meal of her favorite, marshmallow cream and bananas sandwiches on Wonder Bread. She gummed them by the loaf full. When she was done, she licked his hand in appreciation, as she always did. Put her massive head in his lap. Let him scratch the cool leather of her chin.

"Howdy," Leon said to her over and over again, but Miss Pearl wouldn't say a thing. She just rolled her eyes back in her head and looked at him. It was as if she knew. At least that's what Leon thought. Made it hard to look her in the eye.

The next morning when the men came to get her, Leon took Miss Pearl's hat and put it under his bed. He kept it there for a long time. His mama was right. Nobody could forget Miss Pearl. Leon never forgot her at all.

Not even now.

Chapter 8

As they drive past Lucky's RV Round-Up, Jesus waves. "It's an American Dream," he tells Dagmar.

"Sure," she says. "Not my dream, but somebody's."

In her rearview mirror, Dagmar sees the tail end of something parked around back by Leon's office—something large, shiny, and new. Where would he get a rig like that? she thinks. Bob the Round-Up Cowboy seems to wink. Dagmar speeds up. Some things are better left a mystery.

"So what are you doing in Whale Harbor?" she asks Jesus.

"I'm here to save souls," he says in a Jehovah Witness kind of way.

This is not the kind of discussion Dagmar wants to have with a Jesus guy on Christmas morning—or ever. But he leans in. The air feels colder, damper, smells more like dying fish than saltwater. She wishes she'd left the top of the convertible up. His dark hair whips around his face. Makes him look even crazier, more dangerous.

This was just not a good idea, she thinks. Her heart revs.

"Are you ready for life everlasting?" he asks.

Dagmar pretends not to hear. "I'm going to drop you off at The Pink. You can get a bus from there to wherever you're going."

She drives even faster. He knew her name. And is now waiting for an answer. Just ignore it, she thinks. Lack of sleep is making her stomach grind. Her hands sweat. She turns on the radio. Bing Crosby is dreaming of a white Christmas.

Jesus shrugs, sings along for a while. He has a nice voice, a solid baritone.

When Dagmar pulls into The Pink, it's closed. She turns the radio off. From The Pink it's miles away to the interstate, too far to walk. She looks at her watch, nearly 7 A.M. Jimmy Ray is waiting. She looks at the man closely. This is more than a costume.

She has no idea what to do.

Before she can say anything, he says, "You stopped to pick me up because you want to believe in miracles; that's not such a bad thing."

When he says this it feels true, at least a little.

"Well, I just—"

"I can wait here," he says.

"But they're closed until tomorrow."

"Tomorrow is only a day away."

Now, she feels badly. That small-town girl still within her thinks, He's just sad and alone and confused. I'm just overreacting.

"Hang on," Dagmar says. "I'll run you out to the interstate, maybe you can catch a ride there. I just have to stop by and drop these gifts off. It's down the road. Just take a minute."

The voices in Jesus' head are screaming, "Take her now. Do it." Makes his hand shake.

He knows it would be so easy just to lean across the car, snap her neck with one single blow. Run the bridge of her nose through her brain.

Simple. He could do it. Quick. Merciful.

But a man has to have standards. It isn't clear to him yet if Dagmar should be saved. And so, Dr. Ricardo Garcia, firm in the belief that he is Jesus—at least for the moment—sings the hit solo from *Annie*.

"Tomorrow! Tomorrow!

I love ya, Tomorrow! . . ."

And the voices go silent. They hate show tunes.

Chapter 9

Leon never expected Carlotta to leave on Christmas Day, pack up and go without a forwarding address. A two hundred and fifty thousand dollar land yacht is his and Carlotta doesn't even get to know about it, doesn't even get to roll around in its silk sheets, doesn't get to have that Cold Duck and lamé feeling.

He picks up the note that has fallen onto the floor, next to a pile of his dirty socks. The writing is large and lacy. The "Os" are round as powdered mini-doughnuts.

You know where to find me.
Carlotta.

Leon doesn't have a clue. She doesn't have a car. It's pretty far to walk to the interstate. The nearest town is Flamingo. There's a shortcut through the mangroves, so she can have gone there but it seems unlikely. It's not much of a town, smaller than Whale Harbor and well known for its mosquitoes. Black clouds of them swarm both day and night.

Leon suspects she's gone someplace with a mall.

He calls her cell phone again. No answer.

"Leave a message after the tone," a voice says.

"I'm an idiot," he says. "But then, you know that."

Then he presses the "pound" key for "faster delivery." Sits down hard on the waterbed. Waves crash beneath him. He wants to slowly lie back, sleep with the cold water lapping under the heels of his feet. He's not used to staying up all night. He's so tired, everything around him is moving slow and fast at the same time. Everything's a little blurry.

Outside, the sky is turning to india ink. The vapor lights of the trailer court shine through the bedroom skylight. Makes everything look like pink lemonade. That's what Dagmar used to say. When they were first married, she and Leon used to sit on lawn chairs in front of the Airstream and drink pink lemonade with sloe gin. They used to talk about the days when they could have a real kitchen, one with a real stove, not a hot plate. The kind of kitchen you can make tapioca in—even though Dagmar really can't cook. It was just the thought of it. Somebody making tapioca for you makes it a home.

Leon loves tapioca. Mama Po used to make it for him all the time. In poker, *tapioca* is slang for *tapped-out, broke, busted.* Sometimes, Leon thinks his mama was preparing him for what the rest of his life would bring, filling him up with his future.

But, still he loves it. Misses it. And her.

He lies on the bed and watches the stars come out one by one. When the sky looks bruised with them, he dials Dagmar's number. It goes into voice mail immediately.

"It's me," he says and wants to tell her about playing poker with Jesus on Christmas Day, but the more he thinks about it, the queasier he gets. Something about the man's eyes, the suffering in them, makes him feel ashamed.

"Just wanted to say 'hey'."

Hey, I miss you. Hey, I still love you. Hey, I won't screw up again. And hey—Leon can barely think about this part, about standing on the shore holding their young son, Cal, in his arms. His small lifeless body. The riptide.—Hey, I am so damn sorry I want to die.

He wants to tell Dagmar all these things, but it's just too painful. "So, hey," is what he says. "Merry Christmas." Then hangs up. It's the first Christmas without their son, without each other. Dagmar just couldn't forgive him. "You never pay attention," she said when she left. And he knew she was right.

When the moon turns full overhead, Leon drives to the Wal-Mart, Carlotta's note in his hand like a grocery list. Inside the store the light is so bright there are no shadows, no dark places. He walks up and down aisles filled with young men in aprons and bow ties, slicing the tops of boxes with razors, stocking the shelves. Their acne is angry. Their hair, surprised. Leon hardly notices. He's too busy looking, but doesn't think to read the signs, or ask someone.

The store is as large as an airplane hangar; his footsteps echo. Hardware. Auto Repair. Lawn and Garden. The endless tombs of frozen foods. He knows he's getting closer. Two dozen kinds of brownie mix. Fluffy. With nuts. With white chocolate chips. With artificially flavored mint frosting. Fat free. And then he sees it. Shelf stable and the color of chalk. The pearl of fish eyes watching him alone. So he puts it in his cart. Case after case. Tapioca. Premade and ready for anything.

Chapter 10

"This is a Kodak moment if I ever did see one," Jimmy Ray says, beaming. His blue pin-striped suit is immaculate, despite the early hour. His silver hair glints like a department store diamond. He is coconut oil clean.

It's a good day, a strong day, Dagmar thinks, and feels happy. The week before, Jimmy Ray had some trouble getting out of bed. His skin was ashen.

But today, he looks like the old Jimmy Ray, the one who used to boogie woogie with her when she was small. The Jimmy Ray who used to tell her stories of Mardi Gras. Used to tell her about the time he rode in the parade with Louie

Armstrong who was crowned King of Zulu and they both wore traditional blackface, like everybody around them— "Those New Orleans Zulu are white folk after all," he'd say and wink. Used to tell her about Professor Longhair, and the rest of the Blues Jumpers—how they would roller coaster their way through a creole of Caribbean and blues while masked ladies in crinoline spun across the dance floor like peach blossoms in strong wind—"Such lost beauty," he'd always say. That Jimmy Ray: the one filled with life.

"Dagmar, honey, your elf cap is a little crooked."

Jimmy Ray has Dagmar and Jesus posed in front of the Christmas tree. Dagmar is still wearing her green elf cap, which sets off her hair, makes it seem redder than it is. And Jesus, looking a little sleep deprived, is in his sheet. Dagmar adjusts her cap.

"Jimmy Ray, hurry up," she says and put her arm back around Jesus, his bony shoulders. He pulls back slightly. Skittish.

She didn't mean to bring Jesus home to Jimmy Ray for Christmas, but when they pulled into the driveway, Jimmy Ray was standing outside waiting for her. Hands in his pockets, kicking stones with his well-shined shoes. It was a lonely sight. How long he'd been standing in the morning fog was a question too sad to ask. So she didn't.

But when Jimmy Ray saw Jesus and Dagmar he let out a great yelp. "Who you got there, sis?"

Jimmy Ray was laughing so hard he could hardly speak. The sight of Dagmar in her elf cap and Jesus singing show tunes in a sea green Mercedes convertible with its top down was just too much for him to handle. This was not just a chuckle, but eye-watering laugher. Spitting laughter. He could hardly catch his breath, limped a little on the way to the car.

"Sis," he said, "when you said expect a little surprise on Christmas morning, you meant it, darling." Then he turned to Jesus and extended his hand, "Pleased to meet you—"

"Jesus." The man was serious. Jimmy Ray didn't expect that. Up until that moment, he thought the sheet was a joke.

Dagmar shrugged. "He needed a ride."

"You were hitchhiking like that on Christmas?"

"I don't have a lot of choice," Jesus said.

For a moment, the three were unsure of what to say. In the quiet morning, they could hear the snap and pop of Jimmy Ray's police scanners coming from his tiny house. It's a cacophony of violence and mayhem that he seems to find reassuring these days.

After his heart surgery, and conversion to Buddhism, he filled his house with scanners, twenty or more. Each one is locked on to a different frequency: police, sheriff, state police, airports, fire departments, EMS, even FEMA, the Federal Emergency Management Agency, which can provide a lot of drama with all the fires in the Glades and hurricane season. Some are set to pick up Miami. The one in the kitchen has a huge exterior antenna. You can hear all about muggings in Key West on clear days.

"It's the sounds of life," Jimmy Ray told Dagmar when he first put them in. "The world hums with drama. Makes you jingle in your bones."

"You have to stop watching *Cops*."

But Jimmy Ray had a point. His is the only inhabited house for miles in any direction. Gets pretty lonely.

"Look," Dagmar said. "I'm going to run Jesus out to the interstate. I didn't want you to worry."

Jimmy Ray flinched. The idea of sending Jesus packing on Christmas Day, even if he was just a crazy Jesus guy, just didn't seem right. "Maybe we should all have breakfast first."

Dagmar looked squeamish.

"In the spirit of Christmas," Jimmy Ray said.

Dagmar wanted to argue, but, in all the excitement, the caffeine had suddenly worn off. She felt like she'd hit a wall, just wanted to sleep.

"That's mighty nice of you," Jesus said and opened his car door. Shook Jimmy Ray's hand. "I hope this isn't too much trouble."

Jimmy Ray gave a little bow. "No, sir. My pleasure. I got to warn you, though, that I'm a big fan of Mr. Buddha. But if that don't bother you, come on in."

"Not much bothers me anymore," Jesus said.

Jimmy Ray looked at the man, his scarred forehead and hands. His eyes, murky lakes. It frightened him a little, but he tried not to show it. "Well, then," Jimmy Ray said gently. "Let's all have us a little breakfast. Dagmar promised corncakes with real corn and sorghum. Didn't you, darling?"

No, she wanted to say, that's the first I've heard of it. "Huh?" is what she said.

"And while you're at it," Jimmy Ray said, "why don't you give Mr. Trot a call and tell him that we're having Jesus over for breakfast. Maybe he'd like to join us."

Dagmar looked at her watch. 7:02 A.M. Christmas morning. She was pretty sure that Trot, despite his undying love for her, would not find an invitation to breakfast with Jesus of interest at this hour. Of course, sleep-deprived and caffeine-numb as she was, Dagmar was forgetting one major thing—Trot is sheriff. Sheriffs usually like to know when Jesus rolls into their town to celebrate his birthday. However, at that moment, Dagmar was thinking not of Trot, middle-aged law enforcement officer whose mother still buys his underwear, but Trot, the lovesick teenager who stole her gym socks and wore them around for a month. That Trot. The gooney Trot. The Trot she probably should have married.

"I don't understand," she said, but Jimmy Ray didn't hear her. The two men were already walking up the broken sidewalk toward the house—"The Key Lime House," as Dagmar calls it. It's a tiny cottage edged by key lime trees and painted an overripe shade of yellow. Seems to grow from the center of the grove. The sun was rising. A flock of green parrots screeched overhead. A possum ran across the driveway, three babies scrambled after, tumbling on top of each other.

Dagmar was still sitting in the car, confused and yawning.

Jimmy Ray and Jesus stopped at the front door. Turned around.

"You coming, sis? There's breakfast to be made," Jimmy Ray shouted. "And you know that Mr. Trot would love to hear the sound of your voice on a fine morning such as this!"

Jimmy Ray never got over the fact that Dagmar chose Leon over Trot.

"And I'm nothing without my coffee," Jesus chimed in.

Okay, Dagmar thought, they're both crazy.

"Mr. Jesus," Jimmy Ray said, as the two men walked into the house, "I was wondering what influence you think the other Big Dogs had on your philosophy. You know, like Siddhartha, or even Confucius—he had some mighty hep things to say."

And then the two began loudly debating the virtues of polytheism as if they were old friends. Closed the front door behind them.

Dagmar was still sitting in the car.

What Dagmar thought she promised was Waffle House, open 24/7/365, with somebody else cooking and cleaning up. She'd just spent the last few hours cooking for The Dream Café staff and patrons. Since 3 A.M. she'd already fried up twenty-five pounds of sausage and rolled out 288 buttermilk biscuits. Plus, there was a Christmas dinner waiting to be cooked in a cooler in the trunk of her car— turkey and cornbread dressing, mustard greens, sweet potatoes, and a frozen pecan pie that still needed to be baked. What she wanted to do was look at a menu and kick off her shoes.

Jimmy Ray opened the front door. "You coming, child? Breakfast won't make itself."

No sense arguing. She hadn't seen Jimmy Ray this happy in a very long time. Something about the perversity of the situation seemed to bring out the best in him.

So she went in to make breakfast and decided that the phone call, which she knows will feature that ever-hopeful lilt in Trot's voice, could wait.

In the tiny yellow kitchen, Jimmy Ray's refrigerator was filled with things he shouldn't eat, including a quarter shank of country ham, a slab of bacon, and a bowl with a few small brown eggs from Tully, his hen. In the vegetable drawer, there were a few ears of fresh picked corn and some small green tomatoes.

The men were sitting at the dining room table, waiting. She could hear Jimmy Ray tell Jesus about the time the Duke and Duchess of Windsor came to Mardi Gras. He loved that story. "They were the real royalty," he said. "Walked like they were made of glass."

He sounded so happy. So Dagmar fried up the ham, shucked the last ears of corn for corncakes, pulled out the box of pancake mix, and warmed the sorghum. She found three plates that matched and a few oranges from the tree out back for juice. Her back ached. She could feel the veins in her legs. Six hours of cooking, she thought. Six more to go.

When she brought two plates filled with breakfast into the dining room, Jimmy Ray looked surprised.

"You actually *made* breakfast?"

"What did you expect me to do?"

"He thought you were calling the police," Jesus said. "That's why he sent you in there. Breakfast looks good, though." He took his plate from her hand. "Thanks."

"Is that right?" Dagmar looked surprised.

"Pretty easy to figure out," Jesus said.

"Well, why didn't you just tell me?"

She was now whining. Overtired as a child.

Jimmy Ray looked a little sheepish. "Sis, you don't know how to cook. I just figured you'd know I was talking code."

"What do you mean I don't know how to cook?"

Some questions are better left unanswered. That is the one thing that Jimmy Ray knows for sure about women.

Jesus looked up from his plate, a drop of syrup rolled down the corner of his thin lips. His mouth was full of corncakes, but he said. "It's not too bad. I've had worse. Although I've never seen corncakes made with pancake mix. Usually it's made with cornmeal, isn't it? More like a cornbread, I think."

Jimmy Ray was thinking that this was not a good time for a *Zagat* restaurant review.

"Well," Dagmar said, "should I call the police?"

"I would," Jesus said, "but I'm cautious by nature."

Dagmar was still holding a plate filled with food in her hand. For a moment, she appeared to be winding up for a pitch. Jimmy Ray had a panicked Oh-No-Not-Another-Christmas-Day-Massacre look on his face.

"Maybe we should just have some breakfast," he said and quickly took the other plate for himself. "Mmm. Mmm. Looks good."

He tried to sound cheery. But he was, after all, looking forward to pecan waffles and country ham at The Waffle House.

Dagmar was not buying his false enthusiasm. She sat down next to him. Glared. Jimmy Ray shrugged. Jesus tucked into the food with ferocity. He barely chewed, just pushed ham and bacon into his mouth like he hadn't eaten in a long time.

"He doesn't seem to be breaking any laws," Jimmy Ray said. "Honey, if there was an APB out on Jesus on Christmas morning, don't you think I would have heard it?

"I've not even heard a 10–96 in a week."

"10–96?"

Jimmy Ray clucked. "10–96. Psych Emergency. Dagmar, I'd expect a woman of your education to know these things."

"Even I knew that," Jesus said.

Dagmar was not in the mood to be bested by a guy in a sheet, but before she could say anything else Jimmy Ray patted her hand. "Sis, the only serious damage he's doing is to those corncakes."

"Can't fault a man who likes your cooking."

"Let's not labor that point," she said, gave Jimmy Ray a look that could melt cheese. "I guess you're right, though. He seems harmless."

Then Jesus took a long sip of orange juice, swallowed hard, leaned in and said. "But I am Jesus and on some level that is profoundly disturbing. Even to me."

Dagmar and Jimmy Ray exchanged an uneasy glance.

"I guess this still all boils down to whether you believe in miracles, or not."

Dagmar stood up to call the police.

Jesus smiled. "While you're up, a little coffee would help."

"Sure," she said. "Jimmy Ray?"

"No, sis. I'm good."

Dagmar frowned. "I meant would you help me?"

Jesus smiled. "She wants you to go and call the police with her."

"I knew that," Jimmy Ray said, rose from the chair spider-boned, and pained. "I got to stop sitting so long."

In the kitchen, Dagmar dialed 911. Whispered the details. After a few minutes, she hung up the phone.

"You're right. There's no APB on Jesus. He could be harmless. The operator was telling me that apparently you get a lot of this kind of thing on Christmas. Perfectly normal people start speaking in tongues. Too much stress."

"And that's why everybody should be a Buddhist."

"Then the streets would be filled with guys dressed as Buddha and there'd be after Buddha Day sales.

"Anyway, the operator said that unless we can find evidence of brain trauma—you know, like he's been in an accident or had a stroke—they usually remember who they are within a few hours."

"If he doesn't?"

"Then he's probably a flaming nut job. But the police aren't looking for him, so that's some comfort."

"Bottom line?"

"Trot has the day off, and since it's not an emergency, they're not sure when they can send somebody else."

"Well, that's okay. I kind of like him. He's interesting. Got some opinions about the world. You don't see that often."

"Wait a minute, you're the one who thought I should call the police in the first place. Which, by the way, was not very Buddhist of you."

Jimmy Ray shrugged. "Inconsistency is a protected natural right of all us old folks."

"So what do we do?"

"He just seems a little lost."

"I don't know."

The hum of the police scanners filled the moment.

"But he knew my name," Dagmar said.

"Well, how's that a wonder? You got your picture on billboards splayed all over from Venice to Miami. Your name is underneath in bold letters. Any man in his right mind, or not in his right mind, is gonna remember you.

"Maybe you worry too much, gal."

She frowned.

"Besides, I can take care of myself," Jimmy Ray said. "And you, too. Now let's have us a Christmas to remember. It isn't every day that Jesus shows up to party."

"All this talk of Christmas; I thought you were Buddhist."

"Sis, when it comes to presents, I'd be the pope if I had to."

She kissed him on the cheek.

"I love you, sugar," he said; his voice cracked a little.

I love you, Dad, she thought. "What do mean, I can't cook?" she said.

And so now, Dagmar and Jesus are standing in front of the old Christmas tree, fidgety as children, patiently waiting for their photo to be taken. The tree looks just like the one at The Dream Café, silver branches and bubble lights. Uncle Joe bought them both in 1972. They're only slightly tarnished.

"Say salvation!" Jimmy Ray says. And they do. The flash blinds them all.

Chapter 11

Wild Turkey. Tapioca. The fire started without much trouble.

Leon unwraps the boxes of old Christmas lights that he and Dagmar used on their wedding night. Twelve strands. Two hundred and forty bulbs. White and round as tiny snowballs. They were old even back then, and now they're ancient. More than thirty years old. They're left-over from Pettit's All-Stars. After seeing a pictorial about Las Vegas in *Life* magazine, Lettie and Po strung them between the papier-mâché teeth of the entrance.

"If you squint, it looks just like Caesar's Palace," Lettie said. Leon was only four years old, but remembers standing with Lettie and Po in the twilight, squinting, until it was dark and the mosquitoes came thick as clouds.

"Damn it, if you squint it still looks just like Caesar's Palace," Leon now tells Clyde. "Everybody used to say that Pettit's had a certain Vegas feel to it."

Being a six-foot-tall stuffed brown bear, a masterwork in taxidermy, Clyde doesn't respond. Leon's dressed him in an old leather jacket and Ray-Bans. Wants to make him look like Elvis. He's not entirely successful.

"Clyde, where did you put my dang hammer?"

He's also begun to talk to the stuffed bear and, now that Carlotta is gone, is thinking about getting him some wheels so that they can roll down to The Pink on Fridays and pick up women. "That's ladies night," he told Clyde with glee.

Again, no response.

Under the stack of newspapers piled on top of the built-in couch, Leon finds the hammer he's been looking for. "You got to put things back where they belong," he tells Clyde. "Or else things get out of control."

He takes another swig of Wild Turkey. Then files the bottle between Sunday's comics for safekeeping. The extension cord he needs is plugged in, so he yanks it. The TV falls to the floor, bounces, pops, and splinters. Leon doesn't care. Half a liter of Wild Turkey is already gone.

Clyde seems to be scowling.

"If you don't like it," Leon says. "Get your own place."

A load of clothes is spinning in the tiny stacked dryer in

the corner of his bedroom. Carlotta threw everything in the mud. His shoes, socks, even the old jockstrap from high school that he didn't remember he had. When Leon came home, everything he owned was tumbling down the front lawn toward the swamp.

Gators hibernate, he kept telling himself as he waded into the dark water. They are totally asleep. But he knew that wasn't quite true.

Since all his clothes are either wet, or dirty, he stands on top of the waterbed, naked, unsteady, and slightly nauseated from too much of everything—especially himself.

He wants to hang the lights, so he pounds roofing nails into the ceiling, winds the frayed cords around them. Some of the cords are worn thin, so thin they're just bare wires. Leon's so drunk, on the verge of passing out, he doesn't notice. Starlight pours through the roof like cheese through a grater. He keeps on pounding. Wraps the lights around the skylight. Then he opens the latch and pops his head out. The air is salty and thick.

"Nice night," he says to Clyde. "A light chop off the Gulf."

Clyde isn't much when it comes to talking about the weather, either. Leon leaves the skylight open. The cold salt air, its fragrant rot of fish, fills the room.

When all the lights are finally up, all two hundred and forty of them, Leon, still naked, plugs in the extension cord. They snap to life for a moment. The trailer sky is filled with soft stars. The room is cold. Leon's body is all goose bumps and pink flesh, but he doesn't notice. He runs back to the couch, grabs the bottle of Wild Turkey he filed between "Hagar the Horrible" and "Prince Valiant."

"See, right where I left it," he tells Clyde. "Got to have a system."

Whiskey in hand, Leon lies down on the waterbed and stares at the lights and the winking moon that shine down on him through the trailer's open skylight. It reminds him of the smell of White Rain, the cotton candy of Dagmar's hair. On their honeymoon, they came back to the trailer, strung the lights across the skylight, and made love until their lips were rubbed raw.

"It's like we're in the ocean," Dagmar said. "All salty and sweet. Making love under the stars."

Then he thinks of how the ocean turned on him, took Cal. Cal the sun baby. Tall for six. A good swimmer. "My son," he says. He hasn't said those words out loud in so long they creak.

Leon hears sobbing as if it's coming from another room. Tastes salt in his mouth. He wants another drink, damn ocean, but rolls onto his stomach instead. The bottle bobs up and down in his right hand. Facedown in the cool thick plastic of the waterbed, he'd like to smother himself but it seems like too much work.

The lights above his head short and spark. Leon hears the fizzing. Out of the corner of his eye, he sees them flicker, then go out, but he doesn't move. Facedown on the mattress, he opens his eyes and stares into the depths of the waterbed. He can't see a thing. Needs goldfish, he thinks.

The flashes of light remind him of the shooting stars he

saw when he was a kid. They were real shooting stars, a whole family of them. The Flying Zucchinis. Human cannonballs who used to perform in the center of town. Grandfather, grandmother, father, mother, daughter, and son. One after the other, they'd climb into the long black cannon and shoot out over the church parking lot at fifty-six miles per hour.

Their tiny silver jumpsuits. Their tiny silver capes. They were glamorous. They were made of star stuff.

"Wahoo!" he'd scream.

"Make a wish," Mama Po would always say, and he would. He'd wish for a daddy who was spider-legged and softhearted and liked to play baseball.

"Make a wish every chance you get, baby boy," Mama Po said. So he did. Still does.

Across the ceiling, the fire quietly burns along the strands of darkened Christmas lights. Crisscross and sparks. Flames run down the torn drapes and jump across to the piles of dirty clothes. Then there's a loud pop.

Shooting stars, he thinks. Then flips over like a pancake. "Oh," he says when he sees the wall of flame his drapes have become. "I better put that out." But he has no idea how. The fire is spreading quickly. For a moment, he is mesmerized by it. The water in the bed beneath him crests and falls. Somewhere in the back of his brain, Dagmar's voice says, "Pay attention." But, in a Wild Turkey haze, it's difficult to pay attention; the room seems kind, filled with little tiny campfires.

Leon rocks back and forth like an ocean liner.

The fire picks up speed, races across the room, all smoke and spark.

Pay attention, he thinks, but can't. Leon claps his hands like they do on those commercials, trying to applaud the lights back to life. The fire spreads closer and closer to the bed. Smoke fills his mouth, his lungs. Pushes out the air. He coughs hard. Can hardly breathe. His goose bumps are gone. Gagging, he reaches out to his bottle of Wild Turkey. A flame licks his hand like an old dog, and then laps the line of whiskey that spills onto the floor, and then crawls up onto the sheets.

He can hear Dagmar's voice in his head, the midnight whisper of it.

Pay attention.

It is at this point that he thinks of the one thing he hadn't thought of before.

Propane.

The fire slides under the door, and into the galley kitchen. The plastic of the waterbed grows warm underneath him. The tin roof flakes down on his head. He imagines what will happen when the fire spreads to the propane tank.

Like The Flying Zucchinis.

Coughing, his head shakes like maracas. He imagines himself soaring through the air, naked as truth. "She'd be real sorry," he thinks, but the "who" is in question. Smoke and booze has melded Dagmar and Carlotta together in his mind.

She'd be real sorry.

Through the skylight, the cold night air rushes in, fuels the fire. Flames suddenly swell around Leon, singe the hair on his feet, his legs.

"Dang, that smarts."

In his head, Dagmar is now screaming. It's suddenly clear that the fire is past the stage where he can pee on it and put it out—which was more or less his plan a moment ago—so he picks up the blanket that's been lying near his head. Wraps it around his waist and ties it tightly. "Clyde, you're on your own," he shouts and pulls himself onto the roof. Clyde remains stoic. The heat from the fire makes the roof hot. Leon jumps from foot to foot. The waterbed pops, extinguishes the floor.

"Bye-bye, Clyde!"

This is the point where Leon knows he should jump. And he would, but he's afraid of heights. He just remembered that. Another plan ruined by logic. Dang.

"Should have peed on that fire while I had the chance," he says and adds that to the growing list of regrets in his life. Below his feet, he can hear popping, the fire exploding forgotten cans of furniture wax, spray starch. Pretty soon, the propane will go. There's not much time.

He looks over the edge, the ground spins a bit. It's not far to jump, not really. The worst that could happen is that he could break a leg. Or snap my neck, he thinks.

The metal roof is so hot his feet are blistering.

Dagmar's cries come back to him. Pay attention.

So he does. Finally. He tells himself he is a skyrocket, a shooting star better than The Flying Zucchinis—higher, faster. The stars seem so close he could eat them like buttered popcorn.

And so he jumps.

And the propane blows.

And he doesn't forget to make a wish.

Chapter 12

Right before they began cooking Christmas dinner, Jimmy Ray convinced Jesus to put on one of his suits. It was fifty-eight degrees outside, wind out of the North, a cold snap. "Heat's not too good in the house," he told him. "You must be pretty drafty in that thing." He was. It didn't take too much convincing.

Jimmy Ray's walk-in closet looked like the Men's Department at Saks Fifth Avenue. Suit after suit, arranged from blue to gray to black, hung on a long bar across the right wall. Perfectly starched shirts on the left. Racks of shoes at the ready.

"This town must have some dress code," Jesus said.

"Sartorial splendor always gives the impression that you're on your way to a better class of gathering than you're at now," Jimmy Ray said and selected a blue double-breasted pinstripe, a Brooks Brothers he'd bought in Miami a few years back. It was a real classic. Timeless and elegant—but not, however, on Jesus.

Once dressed, the barefoot, tieless man looked a lot like a Mafia hit man on vacation.

"Nearly there," Jimmy Ray said and chose a red Japanese silk tie and matching square. Tied a perfect Windsor knot and arranged the square, just so, in the breast pocket of the fine suit.

"There you go," he said. "What do you think?"

Jesus stared at himself in the full-length mirror. He looked like someone else. Someone he knew, but he wasn't sure who it could be. Made him feel like he was channel surfing though somebody else's life.

"How do *you* think I look?" he said, unsure.

In the right light, the man could have been mistaken for a deranged Italian viscount who once held court at Café Du Monde and fed beignet to a parrot he called "Queenie"—but Jimmy Ray decided that, perhaps, this might not be the right thing to say. So he said, "You look like one of those real executive types, a real mover and shaker. Doctor, maybe."

The word *doctor* made Jesus' hands shake. He hid them in the pockets of the suit coat. "Maybe, I just want to be Jesus," he said. The words rumbled. He looked at Jimmy Ray with those Bible eyes.

At that moment, Jimmy Ray swore he had never seen anybody trapped in so much crazy. Plenty of wild men from back in the day who were hipped up on "horse," or booze, or both—shooting up right onstage—but nobody this crazy who was this calm, and this sober, at the same time. It was hard not to feel sorry for him. Jimmy Ray put his arm around the man's shoulder and gently said, "Son, the shadow of the moon is not the moon."

Jesus looked at him, unblinking, "But the shadow is all we have."

Jimmy Ray had to smile, he couldn't help himself.

"Are you sure you're not a Buddhist?" he said. "I think you're holding out on me."

"I don't think so," Jesus said, "but there's a lot of things I'm not too clear on these days."

So now, the two, resplendent in nearly matching double-breasted pin-striped suits, are in the kitchen making Christmas dinner. Aprons are tied around their bony waists. Jesus is wearing Jimmy Ray's velvet bedroom slippers. Jimmy Ray is in his spit-polished black dress shoes.

Dagmar has been ordered to put her feet up. She is sitting on the couch, asleep, but won't admit it. Every now and then a noise from the kitchen—a laugh, a hoot, the singing of a carol—wakes her and she says, "I'm not asleep." Then falls back into a dream. On the television, Jimmy Stewart is having a wonderful life, more or less. Mostly less.

In the kitchen, however, the two men are chopping onions, country ham, and celery for the stuffing. They work together as if they do this every year. Jimmy Ray lights the gas oven. The jets whoosh.

"It's nice to have company," he tells Jesus. "Not too many folk around anymore."

In Jimmy Ray's neighborhood, blocks of abandoned houses are green with mildew and crumbling back into the sand. They serve as roosts for turkey vultures and the occasional eagle. Herons make nests in the phone lines.

As the men work, Jimmy Ray notices that Jesus has a way with knives. He is precise and quick. The blade moves so easily in his hand, he could be a chef. "Those are nice knives, aren't they?" Jimmy Ray says. "Dagmar got me a set like they have at The Café. They're a little dull, though. I got to make some time to sharpen them."

Jesus looks closely at the knife. It's professional grade. The forged steel blade is large. Sharp or dull, it could do real damage. It reminds him of something. The way it feels in his hand. The weight of it. The power. He gets this odd look on his face, one that Jimmy Ray doesn't trust.

"I think you should know one important fact about me," Jimmy Ray says. "I'm a cautious little Buddhist." Then he lifts up his white apron, his Luger is stuffed in the waistband of his pants. "Just thought you should know."

"I can see that."

"Just so we understand each other," Jimmy Ray says. "Only seems fair." And then he goes back to the chore at hand, tears the cornbread into pieces, adds the vegetables, cracks two eggs, and mixes the stuffing with his hands. In all his years playing the clubs, he's learned that the best way to deal with any kind of crazy is not to deal with it too much. Don't push. Just be clear.

"This is going to be one fine meal," he says.

Jesus, still holding the knife, is watching Jimmy Ray work. Thinking about the gun. Wondering just how quick the old man is.

Jimmy Ray sees the question on Jesus' face. "I'm not going to have to shoot you now, am I?" he asks.

Jesus shakes his head slowly. "Not now, no."

"That's good because those sweet potatoes are not going to peel themselves."

Jesus picks up a sweet potato and peels its tough fibrous skin in one long swirl. Then picks up another. And another. His command of the blade is masterful. Jimmy Ray hums "Amazing Grace."

Nearby, on the counter, collard greens wilt. The frozen pecan pie sweats.

After a while Jesus says, "I think you should know that I don't remember."

Jimmy Ray turns up the heat on the pot of stock that he hopes will reduce down into mighty fine gravy. Flames lick the sides of pot.

"Remember what?"

He turns to see Jesus holding the knife in his hand as if it were a torch. There's no menace in his eyes, just darkness. "Anything," Jesus says. "Before I wound up in Whale Harbor, I don't remember anything at all."

This is not good, and Jimmy Ray knows it. The Luger feels heavy against his ribs. He doesn't want to have to use it. He knows that if he has to fire at this range, he won't miss. He's seen what a Luger can do at close range. Back in 1950, the police escorted him out of New Orleans for shooting a man in self-defense. The force of the shot kicked the man into a wall, and nearly through it. Blew a whole right through the body. The look of surprise on the man's face—Jimmy Ray still remembers it. Remembers it now. Remembers the way the heart kept pumping until the blood was nearly all gone.

Living the blues is a lot harder than singing them, he thinks. The stock, unstirred and unnoticed, begins to boil. Then overflows. Gas flames flicker and spit. Jimmy Ray jumps. "Shoot," he says.

Jesus ducks.

"No. No. I meant 'shoot,' the pot," Jimmy Ray says and quickly lowers the flame. "Not shoot the Jesus."

It's then that Dr. Ricardo Garcia remembers the moment right before he became Jesus. Remembers how peaceful the couple looked in the silk king-sized bed of the American Dream. Remembers how easy it was to drug their drinks at the restaurant and then later overtake them.

In the end everyone welcomes death, he thinks, and smiles.

"You okay?" Jimmy Ray asks. "You doing okay, son? I didn't mean to scare you."

"Sure. I'm just fine," Jesus says and hears Dr. Ricardo Garcia speaking. His voice, always cool and confident, reassures the old man. "Everything is just fine."

"That's good. I'm glad," Jimmy Ray says. Then he remembers, "Hey, you never did tell me what you think of the suit? Is it the real you?"

Jesus looks into Jimmy Ray's old man's yellowed eyes, and can see death there, crouched and waiting. He smiles again and picks up the large stainless mixing bowl filled with stuffing and looks closely at his own image reflected in it—the long hair, the scraggly beard, the crown of thorns scars, the Brooks Brothers pin-striped suit with red silk square, matching tie, and crisp Egyptian cotton shirt with French cuffs.

"It's the real me," he says. "Definitely."

. . .

After Christmas dinner Dagmar has to get back to work, but she hesitates.

"Sis, I'm fine. Really," Jimmy Ray says and looks fine, too, better than he has in a long time, only a little tired.

"Perversity becomes you," she says, shrugs, and drives away uneasy, hoping it's okay, leaving the two men standing on the crushed shell driveway, both in pin-striped suits, waving.

Jesus turns to Jimmy Ray. "Nice girl. Though you should just tell her you're her papa. She knows it, everybody must know it, but it would be a nice gesture anyway."

"You are one spooky dude."

"I know."

Inside Jimmy Ray's key lime house, the scanners hum. It's a quiet night. Every now and then, somebody in Miami calls in a 10–29 for warrants, or a domestic in Key West, but for the most part, the world seems on the edge of soft sleep. The house is hot from all that cooking and Jimmy Ray opens a handful of windows. Their scarf white curtains wave like an aging queen. The two peacocks on top of the roof shed a few plumes. Squawk. Then sleep.

So when Leon's propane tank finally blew, the rest of the world was, for the most part, tumbling into sleep.

Jimmy Ray and Jesus were sitting in front of the television, drowsy and yawning. *It's a Wonderful Life* was on again, the fifth time that day. Jimmy Stewart was again drunk, wild-eyed, and desperate. Ready to jump. Clarence, the angel, again trying to stop him.

"You've been given a great gift, George," Clarence says, insistent. "A chance to see what the world would be like without you."

Even though this movie has been playing nearly non-stop all day long, something about that moment—maybe exhaustion, full bellies, or just the pleasure of silent company—catches the men's attention.

They watch as George Bailey loses his hearing, saves his brother, finds his "Buffalo Gal," and then saves the family business from the ravages of the Great Depression. But, by the time George reaches into his pocket and, amazed to be back in his own life, says, "Zuzu's petals . . . There they are. Well, what do you know about that?"—Jesus has fallen asleep and is dreaming the dreams of Dr. Ricardo Garcia.

His is not a wonderful life.

In the dream, the doctor is in his office in the Ybor City neighborhood of Tampa. The office is in his house, a squat brick two bedroom that sits at the end of the business district, right next to an auto body shop. Out front, a "Family Practice" sign hangs underneath the mailbox. Inside, in his office, there's a framed photo of the former president of Poland, Lech Walesa, and Pope John Paul II skiing together in the Alps. It is the kind of thing sold to tourists. Next to it, his diploma from Harvard Medical School.

Parked in front of the house is a tricked-out canary yellow Olds airbrushed with the faces of rap stars who Dr. Garcia does not know and does not feel the need to know. The car never moves. Dr. Garcia is not sure to whom it belongs, but he doesn't want to cause trouble so doesn't complain.

In his dream, Dr. Ricardo Garcia is who he was back then—a respected member of the community. It's a humid summer morning. He's wearing his favorite cream linen suit, his straw panama hat. He looks as if he's fallen out of time, like a refugee from nineteenth-century Cuba. It's a look he's cultivated though the years.

As he walks down East Seventh, *La Sétima,* he passes the Columbia Restaurant, established in 1905, with its squat Spanish cherubs painted on elaborate tile walls. He also walks past the new condo development where the rich "Club Kids" live, and then past their clubs with names like "Indigo" and "Inferno." He walks past El Sol's Handmade Cigars, Phat Katz Tattoo parlor, the Celtic Knowledge Shoppe whose sign offers a "special on aura readings today only," and then past the housing project that anchors the outskirts of this neighborhood that was once considered a ghetto for Cuban refugees who worked all hours of the day and night at *Cuesta-Rey* Cigar. Even in his dreams, as Dr. Ricardo Garcia walks this street, it is mired in history and sorrow. He waves at his neighbors, even the ones he doesn't know. Most wave back.

When he reaches S. Agliano and Sons Fish Company,

he stops in to inquire about an ancient aunt who was his patient. "Better," the man says. Al Martino is on the stereo singing "Volare."

"Sometimes the world is a valley of heartaches and tears," the lyrics wail.

Then, even though it is a dream, he crosses the street to eat his breakfast as he did every morning, with the cigar-smoking old men at *La Tropicana*.

As soon as he walks into the café, just as it was in real life, the waitress brings him his usual—Cuban coffee and a guava turnover. He says grace, as he always does, and then listens to the men argue about Cuba, the old country.

Sitting with the old men was good for business. One by one, they came to him, and later brought their wives, grandchildren, and mistresses. But he never said much because every time he did, one or another of the old men would tease him.

"You call yourself a Cuban?"

Which of course Dr. Ricardo Garcia did. But isn't. So he had to be careful.

The dream is so real that it makes his heart beat faster. As he eats the sweet pastry, he can taste it. The old men speak of nothing in particular, slip in and out of English, as was their custom. They are sitting next to a mural of themselves that was painted on the wall a few years back. Life and art merge.

La Tropicana and the old men are the bones of the history of the neighborhood, a history that Dr. Garcia had hoped to be a part of. And he is thinking this while he dreams. Thinking about how he misses the gossiping old men, and the trolley that runs down the street, and the wrought iron terraces, and the even the Club Kids.

Then the dream shifts.

Suddenly, the one Dr. Ricardo Garcia calls "The First" is sitting across from him. Laughing. Just as he did the night of his death.

The First was a male nurse who worked at the hospice. Angelo. Forty-three years old. Divorced four times. Gold tooth, burly. Always smelled of meatloaf.

He didn't deserve salvation.

He'd come for a B-12 shot to "pep him up," but when he saw the doctor's framed photograph of the pope and Poland's president skiing in the Alps together he said, "Wanna hear a joke, Doc?" Didn't wait for an answer, but continued on. "Two Polish hunters are driving through the countryside to go bear hunting. They came to a fork in the road where a sign read 'BEAR LEFT.' So they went home."

And then he said, "Heard about the Polish hockey team? They all drowned during spring training."

So Angelo had to die.

And now he's in the dream.

"Hey, Doc," he says. "You didn't have to get so sore. You can have just taken out the word *Polish* and inserted *Dan Quayle*. It's dated, but it still works."

Then the dream ends. Leon's propane tank blows.

The explosion rattles the windows. A handful of oranges fall off the trees.

"Almighty!" Jimmy Ray says, still asleep. Out of reflex,

he pulls the Luger from his pants and shoots into the ceiling fan. Then through the roof. The roosting peacocks trill and squawk. The ceiling fan flames, comes to a halt. Bits of plaster snow. The TV snaps off, as does the lights. The scanners are silent. The room is smoke dark.

Jesus is breathing hard and sweating. Jimmy Ray falls back onto the couch. He tosses the gun onto the floor, as if it's suddenly too hot.

"I could have killed somebody," he says, distraught. Holds his head in his hands.

Jesus quickly tucks the fallen gun into his pants. The metal is hot against his skin. Burns. Doesn't matter, he thinks. Pain is good. Pain is right. Pain is all we have in this world. Pain is the only one true gift.

"You okay?" Jimmy Ray says.

"I'm okay," Jesus says. His voice is calm, reassuring. "I'm fine."

Jimmy Ray has that old man's shake to his voice. "I was dreaming," he says. "I was just dreaming, man. Didn't mean no harm."

The hot metal of the gun makes Jesus' skin blister. He likes that. "I know," he says. "You're a good man. A man deserving of God's grace."

In the distance, black smoke billows like storm clouds, clouds the moon once more.

"You are a man bound for salvation."

Chapter 13

It's nearly an hour after the explosion before Trot arrives on the scene. Dispatch tracked him down in Miami, at his mother's house, stuck to the vinyl of her sofa covers making small talk with a rat-faced man who could soon become his new father. He's never been so happy to be called into work. At least until he heard the details.

"Mayor says there's not much left of Leon."

Trot doesn't know what to say.

"You still there, Sheriff?"

"What about the girl?" he says. Can't even say Carlotta's name.

"There's just not much left of anything. You better come."

By the time Trot arrived on the scene, the fire was out. There were still some embers, so he parked across the creek from the trailer. Stayed in his squad car. He just couldn't seem to get out and take a look at what was left of Leon. And maybe Carlotta, too.

Probably Carlotta, too.

The idea of Carlotta being dead made Trot's legs go numb, his chest tight, breath shallow. When he first arrived, he opened the car door, slightly, for a moment. The night air rushed in, propane heavy and hot. It smelled like BBQ, which unfortunately allowed Trot to imagine, in great detail, what it would be like to be blown up. The surprise of it. Body parts like confetti. He nearly threw up.

Trot closed the car door quickly. Sweat slid down the side of his face, even though the night was chilly. He started to shake. Over and over again, he imagined Carlotta falling from the sky like confetti, then sequins—and then like sparks from a bottle rocket on the Fourth of July.

"Sheriff!"

"Over here! Look!"

Trot rolled down the car window and squinted. Across the narrow creek, he could see that there were still a handful of townspeople standing around the burned trailer. They were muddy from fighting the fire. Some were holding hoses. Some still stamping down cinders.

"Go home," he shouted. "Show's over." Then rolled the window back up again.

It wasn't what the crowd expected to hear. A chorus of voices rang out in the night.

"Aren't you going to take a look?"

"Don't we get a medal or something?"

"We put it out!"

"Don't you want to see?"

Trot flashed his high beams and rolled down the window again.

"I can see," he said. Rolled it back up.

"I mean up close," a woman shouted. Her voice reminded Trot of that clicking sound chalk makes when someone is writing on a blackboard. "Trot? Shouldn't we be getting out of the car?"

Chalky, all-business, and stern—Trot knew he knew this woman, but couldn't remember her name, even though he was pretty sure he'd known her all his life. Not my mom, he thinks, she's in Miami.

"Trot?"

She gave his name so many syllables it was like she was singing a scale. Yes, Trot knew her. Knew her chalkboard singsong voice as well as he knew his own. Knew her pink hair and her pink housedress. He just couldn't seem to remember her name. Or anybody's. Shock, he thought.

Not good.

"Trot, honey, isn't it part of your job to get out of your car?" the woman said.

Trot turned his headlights off. "No, ma'am."

There was some mumbling in the crowd. "Best friends," a man's voice said. "They were best friends."

"Oh," the singsong chalkboard pink woman said. "That's right. Always mooning over that little Dagmar."

Then the handful of people mumbled away.

Best friends, Trot thought. Leon. Me. Best friends forever.

The words made him feel bad. He hadn't really thought much about Leon until that moment, but it was true. They fished and lied and drank and lied and hated each other and lied and envied each other and lied and knew when to shut up and when to talk and when to lie—and they both seemed to always fall for the same woman. If that isn't real friendship, what is?

And Dagmar.

Who's going to tell Dagmar?

Trot knew the answer. It was his job, of course, but he hoped the singsong chalkboard pink woman got there first.

Trot shone the bright lights again. Kept them on for a minute, or two. The "scene" was impressive. There was a crater where the trailer once stood. Somebody did die, that was clear. Under the blue white light of the high beams, Trot could see a huge lump of something. A body. Maybe two. Probably two.

Not like confetti at all, he thought. Or bottle rockets. Or sequins. He turned the headlights off again. Closed his eyes and waited for the world to stop spinning.

A few minutes later, Bender, the mayor, dressed in a Hawaiian print bathrobe and high-top red tennis shoes, walked up carrying a bottle of cognac. He smelled of smoke. His eyebrows were singed, as was the hair on his hands. Bags of peanuts were stuffed into his pockets. Putting the fire out was his idea, so he'd gone back to The Pink to get everyone a beer. Then the phone rang.

"They were best friends, after all," Mrs. Sitwell, the singsong chalkboard pink woman said. Mrs. Sitwell was Trot's former fifth-grade teacher. "Our little Trot needs a friend right now," she said in that all-knowing fifth-grade teacher kind of way, so Bender traded the six packs for cognac. VSOP.

Bender taps gently on the window. There's no response. He remembers Carlotta and Trot dancing just the night before. Their shy grace. Then remembers a quote from Hemingway, "If two people love each other, there can be no happy end to it," then taps on the window again, a little harder.

Trot opens his eyes and rolls the window down. Sighs. Bender's red and green Jell-O–dyed hair glows in the moonlight.

"You know, I think it was inevitable that Leon would explode one day," Bender says gently. He's always saying things like that. He has a PhD.

"Why are they making martinis?" Trot asks.

It takes Bender a moment to understand what Trot is saying. Bender's bathrobe features tiny grass-skirted hula dancers dancing in martini glasses holding even tinier cocktail shakers in their minuscule hands. Bender leans into the car and turns on the interior light. Trot doesn't blink.

Shock, Bender thinks.

"The robe," Trot says. "Why are they making martinis?"

Bender runs a hand through his Jell-O hair. "It's a protest against the sociological implications of the stereotype of women in paradise. As a culture, we tend to see raw native beauty as lacking in refined skills. The martinis represent a sophisticated outlook."

Trot looks confused.

Bender translates. "Big hair does not mean tiny brains."

A look of profound revelation crosses Trot's face. "That's the real truth of the world, isn't it? The higher the hair, the closer to heaven."

Then he rolls the window up and closes his eyes again.

Bender pulls the foil from around the cork of the cognac and takes a long swig.

It is going to be a long night, and Bender knows it. So he sits on the hood of the squad. Settles in.

Bender is the kind of man who knows when to push and when not to. He's been mayor, chief bartender, and self-appointed moral conscience in Whale Harbor for more than a decade. Like most in town, he's an outsider. A marine biologist by trade, he'd worked on the *Calypso* with Jacques Cousteau; his wife, Simone; and their son, Philippe.

He calls this part of his life "The Pirate Years." And, after a few cognacs, he will tell the story of how it came to an end one New Year's Eve in Mexico.

"There was a full moon and it was quite balmy, a remarkable evening," he always begins. "We were anchored beneath the cliffs of the Guadeloupe, home to hundreds of elephant seals. Snouts like real elephants.

"It was mating season. When the bull seals trumpet, your knees shake, the ground shakes."

And then, always at this point in the story, Bender "trumpets" himself as if suddenly turned into a seal looking for a mate. The sound is thunderous. Somewhere midtrumpet his voice would arch, and then crack.

Most look away when he does this. He's usually sweating by this point, no matter what the season. The heat of the story always overwhelms him.

"I could see these huge ancient beasts crying out for love. I wanted to join them. So, I did."

Jumped overboard. Never returned to the boat. Blames it on the moonlight.

"I just fell in love with the idea of love," he always says. "There was a pretty one. I still swear she was a mermaid. 'Selkie' they call them. My sweet selkie."

Then he sighs so deeply his bones seem to rattle.

"Trot?" he says now, presses his face against the windshield and squints. "VSOP. Did I mention it was VSOP? Aged twenty years? The good stuff?" He shakes the cognac in his hand and then barks like a papillon. It is a butterfly-eared yip. Bender is working on a new theory about getting in touch with one's "inner dog." He's still trying to figure out what breed his is. So he yips the papillon yip again, but it feels a little "too frilly."

"Did I mention that this cognac is the stuff dreams are made of?"

"I'm on duty."

"And I'm mayor."

"That's true."

"I could order you."

"You could."

"Or you could just open up."

There is obviously no sense in arguing. Trot slowly leans across the squad and opens the passenger door. Bender rolls off the hood, gets into the car. He smells like smoke and well water, that rotten egg smell. Hands Trot the cognac.

"Cheers," Bender says, but his voice is not cheery at all, just sad. He watches Trot take a long sip.

"Burns," Trot says, a beer man by habit. The cognac makes him cough.

"You've called for backup?"

"County medical examiner. Dispatcher says it will be an hour, or more. Gang thing." Trot takes another long pull, then coughs again.

"You want to talk about it?" Bender says. His voice is men's movement smooth.

Trot hopes beyond all good reason that the "it" in question is "baseball," but knows he can't be that lucky.

"Sometimes it's good to talk about it," Bender says again.

"I'm fine."

"Can't always keep things all bottled up."

Trot wants to explain that keeping things bottled up is good. Without bottles there'd be beer all over the refrigerator—but he just shrugs. "I'm fine."

Bender leans over and says, "You know, I have some expertise with matters of the heart."

Suddenly, the song "Feelings" pops into Trot's head.

Makes him want to pepper spray himself. Please change the subject, he thinks over the din of the seventies slow-dance croon.

Feelings, wo-o-o feelings . . .

Bender touches him on the shoulder says, "Son, I have seen a selkie on a moonlit night and heard her call. I know that once that happens a man can never be content to be mortal again."

And when he says this Trot can feel Bender's sorrow in his own heart and he thinks of Carlotta standing on the street in the rusted moonlight waiting for him. Thinks of how he ran to her, how she smiled. How she made him feel greater than himself.

"Damn," he says.

"Man can't help himself." Bender sounds wistful. "These selkies, they bewitch."

"That they do."

Trot takes a sorrowful pull from the bottle; a third of it is now gone. Passes it back to Bender.

"You know," Bender says. "There's only one cure on earth when a selkie steals your heart."

Trot knows. He's heard the story of Bender's last voyage on the *Calypso,* or "Collapse-O" as many call it, so many times it's as if he's lived it himself. And so, like bull seals in the moonlight, he trumpets as he has heard Bender do so many times. It is more of a howl, really. His voice wavers and cracks.

And Bender joins in.

And so, about an hour later, when the State Highway

Patrol and the county medical examiner finally make it to the scene, they find the two men sitting in the moonlight like huge ancient seal lions—drunk, hoarse, and howling.

"Got to love a small town," the medical examiner says, mostly to himself.

Chapter 14

In the garage, the ancient fuse box is nearly rusted shut. The door crumbles when opened. The fuses are made of glass. There are no spares. They're hard to come by. So last year Jimmy Ray rigged the box so that it overrides the breaker. He felt this was an ingenious idea unless, of course, the entire fuse box burns out.

Now, of course, the entire fuse box is burned out.

"Shoot," Jimmy Ray says. Jesus holds the flashlight as the old man stares at his handywork. The flashlight battery is weak. The light flickers. There are no spare batteries, either.

"Shoot. Shoot. Shoot."

The word sounds like a sneeze. Jimmy Ray spits on the ground, jiggles the fuses. "Come on, just a little juice," he pleads, but nothing happens. "Dang phones are out, too," he prattles on. "Dagmar got me one of those portable ones. Base got to be plugged in for it to work. Shoot."

Jimmy Ray is mumbling in chorus with the voices that are sliding in and out of Jesus' head. Reality is a little fluid for him right now. He's going in and out of being Jesus like a Yugo with gears that slip. The voices whisper, buzz like gnats. Make his ears itch. Jimmy Ray's lost Luger is still stuffed into the back of his trousers. And it's still hot. His skin is burned, blistered, and peeling, which makes him want to scratch his butt.

ONLY MONKEYS SCRATCH THEMSELVES IN PUBLIC, he tells himself over the psychotic rambling chorus in his brain.

And then there's Jimmy Ray, and all his mumbling.

Jesus, as they say, is pulled a little too tight right now. So he snaps.

"Annunciation is an important social skill," he screams, exasperated. Shrill as a smoke alarm. Then pounds his head with his fists. Light from the flashlight bounces off the ceiling of the garage, its wall.

Everybody—voices included—stops talking.

Jimmy Ray turns around, nice and easy, cocks an eyebrow. "Sorry, son," he says. "You're absolutely right. I'll speak up." Then goes back to jiggling fuses.

The sudden quiet makes Jesus feel calm again. "Is it dead?"

"And buried," Jimmy Ray says and slams the fuse box door shut, which causes it to fall off its rusted hinges and thud to the ground.

For a moment, the two men stand in a circle of flickering light and stare at the crumpled door lying on the dirt floor of the garage. The fallen door is just another sobering reminder that in the never-ending struggle of man versus house—the house always wins. It's a basic fact of life. And no matter how crazy a man is, he knows this, although he hates to admit it.

"Shoot," they both say in unison.

Outside the garage the night is still. The air is damp with rust. Jesus turns off the flashlight, and the two men watch the fire burn in the distance.

"Man," Jimmy Ray says. "I wish I knew what that was. Looks close to town. Could be The Pink. That be a shame."

Just then a hungry raccoon makes a run for the chicken coop. Triggers the battery-powered security floodlight. The light slaps on, a startled sun. Both men jump. The raccoon runs away.

Jimmy Jr., Jimmy Ray's rooster, thinks it's morning. Crows. The night is suddenly filled with the sounds of fowl love. The rooster is a randy sort. His combs are flared. He's flying around the coop with great determination. All he needs is a splash of Brut. Tully, Dahlia, and the rest of the Rhode Island Reds flap wildly to get away. The rooster looks like a flamenco dancer sidestepping his way into them. He spreads his wings and tail feathers, struts, and makes a booming sound.

It's impressive, but the hens want no part of it. They nip at his neck with their sharp beaks. Some draw blood.

"Women. They are a wicked species," Jimmy Ray says, laughing.

The security light goes out and the two men are in the dark again. "Want some hooch?" Jimmy Ray says, takes the flashlight from Jesus and fixes it on an old box marked "*Playboy* 1977–78."

"Only place I can hide it. Dagmar never thinks to look here. Too much like work."

He blows off the dust. Pulls out a mason jar filled with pink liquid.

Jesus holds the jar up to the dim light. "Looks like antifreeze."

"Passion fruit," Jimmy Ray says. "Stuff grows wild as kudzu around here. "

Jesus is suddenly skittish. "You know, it's called passion fruit in honor of the Crucifixion."

"That it is," Jimmy Ray says. "And I can guarantee if you drink too much it will surely crucify you. It'll hoodoo the Hoodoo Man."

Jesus takes a sniff. "Smells like antifreeze, too."

Jimmy Ray laughs. "I like to think of it as 'crisp,' but with a mouthfeel that is surprisingly chewy and a lighter fluid finish with a slightly floral nose."

As Jimmy Ray speaks it is clear, even to him, that he has spent a little too much time hanging out with those Atlanta CIA chefs at The Dream Café.

"Besides," he says, "nothing else to drink in the house."

"Understood."

Jesus raises the jar to his lips, but before he can drink, Jimmy Ray catches his hand.

"Word of warning, son. I wouldn't gulp if I were you. Man lost all his hair once like that. Just dribble a little into your mouth and roll it around until the burning sensation stops.

"It's a mighty powerful year."

Jesus looks a little frightened, takes a tentative sip. In a matter of seconds his eyes water. He is shaking as he hands the jar back to Jimmy Ray. "I see what you mean about the secondary floral notes," he says. His voice sounds as if it has been squeezed through cheesecloth.

"Grand, isn't it?" Jimmy Ray laughs, wipes the jar on the sleeve of his suit, and takes a sip.

Jesus coughs. "It's something."

Jimmy Ray often thinks of bottling his hooch. Call it "White Zinfandel" with a Vargas-type girl on the label. Appellation: The Dream Café. But it would need a screw top. Jimmy Ray tried to cork it once; cork melted.

"I can make a fortune with this stuff. I know it," he says. "I can see everybody in America swigging Passion Fruit Hooch, making Hooch martinis, Hooch spritzers with little umbrellas. I do believe that if we put a southern boy in the White House again, Passion Fruit Hooch would be served at all the fancy heads of state dinners.

"I can even see the motto . . . 'Save your hair! Sip, don't slurp!'"

After another sip Jesus can see it, too. "Then why don't you do it?" he says.

Jimmy Ray shakes his head. "I'm too old, son. I'm planning my farewell, not my comeback, tour."

Then he slaps Jesus on the back like an old friend, which, even in his cyclone of crazy, makes Jesus feel guilty because he knows, eventually, after Dagmar, he is probably going to kill the old man. It's just what he does, natural as breath. Bowlers bowl. Killers kill.

Or, as he prefers to think about it, "saviors" save.

And some people have a problem with salvation. He's just hoping Jimmy Ray isn't one of them. He'd hate to lose the man's friendship. Can't remember if he's ever had a friend before, but he certainly likes this one. Likes his easy Buddhist way.

For a long while, the two men sit together on the back steps of the tiny key lime house and watch the fire burn itself out in the distance. Every now and then, they skip stones off the rooster's comb and make him leap, which triggers the security light, and avian lust, again, kicks into high gear.

The hooch makes the voices in Jesus' head stay silent. He suddenly feels lucky, just like he used to in the old days when he was a respected man sitting at *La Tropicana* with the other respected men. Talking. Just talking.

But there are twelve reasons why he can never go back. Most, like the rough trade boys, can never be traced to him. A few, however, were sloppy.

Suddenly he feels remorse. "I miss my old life," he says sadly and hears the voice of Dr. Ricardo Garcia speaking.

"I know what you mean, son."

Out of reflex, Jimmy Ray's hand lightly touches the scar across his own chest, across his heart. The scar from his surgery. It's a sad gesture, filled with longing.

That's when Jesus decides to kill him sooner, rather than later. Out of friendship. Relieve the old man's suffering. He's a good man and he deserves it.

The gun against his spine is still a little warm.

Salvation is at hand, Jimmy Ray, Jesus thinks. Prepare yourself.

"Bowlers bowl," he says, as if it explains why he's about to take the Luger and blow a hole clean through Jimmy Ray's aristocratic, although somewhat battered, heart.

"Bowlers bowl," Jimmy Ray says, rolls the phrase around in his mouth like Passion Flower Hooch.

Jesus pulls back the suit jacket slightly. On the count of three, he thinks.

Oblivious, Jimmy Ray runs a hand though his perfect marcel hair. "I've never heard 'Bowlers bowl' before," he says. "How about this one—'Ultimate reality has a unified form.'

"I got that off that *Daily Zen* website last week."

The idea gives Jesus pause. He makes a note to himself: never kill a Buddhist—too much obtuse chitchat.

"Bowlers bowl," he says again, this time with a weighty dose of dread. "Doesn't that scare you even a little? Just the idea of it?"

Jimmy Ray seems bemused. "Son, groups of men in matching shirts always scare me." Then he laughs, and the mood is ruined, the moment lost.

It is then that Jimmy Ray reaches over and pats Jesus' back out of friendship. His hand accidentally touches the gun. Both the men feel it. The gun doesn't surprise Jimmy Ray. He's already figured that Jesus picked it up from the floor. He just wondered when it would make its debut. He's a crazy Jesus fella after all, and that's what crazy Jesus fellas do.

Jesus, on the other hand, is not taking it so lightly. This complicates matters. He thought this would be easy; hoped thirteen was his lucky number. Now, there would probably be a scene. A struggle. Maybe even a mess. Ten was messy. Ten was a nightmare of mess. Ten woke up in the middle. Such a fuss Ten made.

He hates it when they make a fuss. "Are Buddhists fussy?" he says.

Jimmy Ray can see the look of deep concern on the man's face. "Not usually, depends on the topic." He takes another swig of Passion Fruit Hooch and pats the gun again, this time on purpose.

"By the way," he says, "I used my last ammo clip in the assassination of the ceiling fan. I think you should know that. Save yourself some trouble later down the road."

And then, in one swift fluid move, Jimmy Ray pulls the Luger out of the younger man's pants. The whole thing happens so fast, so smoothly, that Jesus doesn't even have a chance to react.

"Thanks for keeping it safe," Jimmy Ray says and twirls the gun around his thumb like a Wild West star.

"How'd you do that?" Jesus squeaks.

"Well," Jimmy Ray says, "you know what they say—'Bowlers bowl.'"

Jesus looks confused.

Jimmy Ray shakes his head and says gently, "Son, just 'cause I'm old doesn't mean I'm not a player. Once a player. Always a player."

Then Jimmy Ray yawns, hands the gun back to Jesus. "The only thing this is good for now is stirring brown sugar in your oatmeal tomorrow morning. You like oatmeal?"

"I'm not sure."

"That's good enough for me."

Jimmy Ray goes back into the house and leaves Jesus sitting alone on the back steps.

Things to do tomorrow, Jesus thinks: grant Jimmy Ray his final rest; blow town before that rube Leon runs the plates on the Dream.

Dr. Ricardo Garcia is now back for good.

Chapter 15

After several pots of coffee, Sheriff Trot Jeeter, not too drunk anymore, pulls up to The Dream Café. His heart is racing. Maybe it's from the caffeine, or maybe from too much confusion. The medical examiner searched the scene and found no specific signs of Carlotta. No red sequin dress. No high heel shoes. No woman's clothing at all, in fact. The bones left look a little too long, a little too large to belong to a woman.

"There's a chance that she left before the explosion," he explained, "but it's difficult to tell. The fire burned hot. All that's left is a lump of something that is more or less human. A one big lump. And a pair of sunglasses nearby. And what appears to be a fragment from a black leather jacket.

"It's a pretty hairy mess."

"How long till we know if it is one body, or two?"

"Don't know. Got a backlog. 'Tis the season."

"Well, what do *you* think? Could it have been two people?"

"Sure. They could have been in the throes. Won't know until we can run all the bone fragments for the DNA."

Trot winced. "Thanks," he said, and unfortunately now has a striking visual image of the last thing on Earth he wanted to think about—Leon and Carlotta "in the throes."

And now, he gets to talk to Dagmar.

Merry Christmas, he thinks.

The Dream Café's parking lot is nearly full. He finally finds a space next to a new Lexus with gold wire rim hubcaps and an expired Illinois license plate. Takes a moment to write a ticket for it. Places it securely under the gold-plated wiper blade.

Damn snowbirds, he says under his breath, but thinks about the old days when tourists were everywhere and the Ferris wheel, with its blue and red lights, still ran. He and Dagmar were stuck on the top of it one summer. So he kissed her. And she kissed him back. Promised to love him forever.

It suddenly seems like so long ago. He tears up the ticket. Writes up a warning, instead.

When Trot opens the door to The Café, the place is filled.

Plates chatter like teeth. The girls are between shows. Everyone seems to be eating,

Doesn't anyone know it's still Christmas?

The lights are dim, but the place is cheerful, not dark. The air is fragrant with Today's Special, which is discreetly written on a board next to the door—apple wood smoked turkey with *pommes frites* of Yukon Gold potatoes twice fried in virgin olive oil and sprinkled with Gilroy garlic and fresh rosemary. Busch beer $1.29 on tap.

Turkey, french fries, and beer, he translates. His stomach growls. Man, I should have had some dinner.

Just a few feet away, he spots Dagmar sitting at a high top table near the bar with a large plate of french fries smothered in catsup. He watches her for a moment. She's drinking a glass of milk, and reading the *Wall Street Journal* in the dim light. You'll ruin your eyes, he thinks and shakes his head. Old habits are hard to break. She looks fourteen again, hair piled up like whipped cream. He tries not to think about her that way, like the girl he once loved, but it is difficult. He watches her as she makes notes in the *Journal* with a red pen and thinks of what Bender said, "High hair don't mean tiny brains."

She sees him and smiles. Waves him over.

He takes his hat off when he gets to the table. "Sheriff Jeeter," she says sweetly. Pronounced the word *sheriff* as if it is some sort of joke between them. No disrespect intended, it's just that the words seem too formal to say without a trace of a laugh. "I was going to call you tomorrow. Come have one of these *pommes frites* with an American-styled tomato reduction; and I'll tell you about our Christmas visitor, and you can tell me what you think about this new trend in mutual funds. The *Wall Street Journal* did a feature on it, but I'm not convinced."

Trot feels a bead of sweat run down the center of his spine. If she touches me, he thinks, I can't do it. He walks over, unsmiling. "Dagmar," he says, gently, still amazed at how sweet her name is on his lips. "We might have a problem with Leon."

"What's he done this time?"

He notices she has a small milk mustache. He reaches across and picks up a napkin from the bar, touches it to his own lips. "Milk," he says and then hands her the napkin.

She laughs, wipes her upper lip. "Better?" He nods. "Now, what's this about Leon?"

She looks so happy sitting there he hesitates. There is really no good way to say this, he thinks. So he says it the best way he can.

"Leon appears to have been fried up like a fritter."

Chapter 16

Even though it's Christmas, and nearly midnight, they're still swapping and shopping on the Power Possum AM. A caller named Al sounds as if he's in his twenties. He's offering a blue fleck metal pickup with *Playboy* mud flaps and most of its engine.

"1994. Nearly new," Al says, his words slur. Al didn't see the ditch, so it's going for $350 cash, or the in-kind services of a DUI lawyer.

"They only let me get one call and this one was it," he says. "So if you want it, just go on and call Sheriff Jeeter. He's got the keys to impound."

Trot's name makes Dagmar cry all over again. Mascara runs muddy down her cheeks. She wipes them with the back of her hand. The night is unseasonably warm. Damp, like sweaty palms.

Trot took her out to what was left of Leon's place. She took a bottle of sloe gin with her from the bar. And her own car. She wanted some space to let it sink in. It wasn't just Leon's place. It was their place. Leon. Dagmar. Cal.

Yellow caution tape rings the charred trailer. A pink flamingo from the garden is a puddle. Some of Leon's things lay scattered on the grass, including the framed photocopy of Grover Cleveland on the thousand-dollar bill. He'd won it in Vegas the weekend they'd married.

"It's like our wedding picture," he told her when he hung it up on the wall.

Dagmar felt a wave of regret when she saw it. Made her feel like some things are never over. Husbands are shadows you can't shake.

Then she thinks about Trot. Poor Trot. Feels ashamed.

"There's a brand-new rig over at the Round-Up," he said when they first arrived. "Any idea where a guy like Leon would get something like that?"

That's when Dagmar slapped him. Something about the way he said "guy" set her off. He wouldn't even cross the creek. "You can see all you need to from here," he said, still in his car.

Dagmar had never seen Trot like that before, saying all kinds of cop things.

"The call came in at 8:34 P.M."

"The medical examiner will have a determination of the time of death sometime in the near future."

"Why are you being such a jerk?"

"I'm not," he said quietly. Then pulled away without saying another word.

"Sorry, Trot," she says, now, two hours later.

She's sitting in the middle of what Trot called "the scene," sitting on a faded lawn chair in that pile of charred rubble that used to be her front porch. She's listening to a radio that someone left nearby. She's not sure what she's listening for, or why, but the scratchy sound makes her feel less alone. The lawn chair is bent, the blue plastic webbing slightly melted. When she cries, it rattles beneath her. She takes a sip from the bottle of sloe gin. Spits it out. She doesn't drink anymore since Cal died, doesn't want to depend on anything ever again—not booze, not love. Especially, not love.

"Love's a cakewalk," Leon told her before she left.

She understood what he meant. You run in circles until you're the only one left. Then you win. But you're alone. Everything you love either dies, or leaves, and you're sitting alone in a wobbly chair with music playing too loud, too fast. That's why she'd sworn off love for good. "I'm beyond love," she's told everyone. "Don't need it, don't want it." But still wears her wedding ring.

"To ward off wandering eyes," she tells the dancers, but they don't believe her.

Sometimes at night they see Leon sitting in the parking lot in his Pimp Daddy Caddy with the top down, the lights off, and the motor humming. Even though the mandarin orange paint job nearly glows in the dark, they point him out to her. But Dagmar always says she doesn't see him and goes back to the tables, teases couples, and buys a round of drinks for the ones celebrating their anniversaries.

She does, of course, see him. Everybody knows it.

Sometimes when she closes up for the night and the air is thick with stale smoke and Four Roses, she stands in the darkness watching him watch her.

It is at those moments that she thinks of what they had—not the bad things, not the drunken fights, not the lies they told between them—but she thinks of the quality of his love, the gentleness of it. How he'd hold her during thunderstorms so she wouldn't be afraid. How he wondered if Mama Po and Miss Pearl were together in heaven still doing that lovely, silly routine.

"Can you say 'howdy' for the folks, Miss Pearl?"

Late at night, watching him watch her—so close, so far away—she always remembers Leon with grace, remembers him as a man who makes wishes on fountains and rainbows and the smoke of candles. Remembers him as a man who wished for things that never seemed to come true.

And now he's gone for good.

Her mouth feels like a maraschino cherry: too sweet, redder than real. This stuff is horrible, she thinks and puts the bottle of sloe gin next to her and turns her attention to the transistor radio. She gives the lighted dial another turn. Radio signals slip off the Big Dipper and collide into dead stars. They hum, hiss, and pop with the static of words and music. Sound like an alien love song.

She's looking for something, something that can't be

swapped or shopped on Power Possum AM, something that's all about alligator love under a pink lemonade moon in tin sky. For a moment, the radio latches on to a clear signal.

"Do you believe in God?" a voice says.

She stops a moment. "I'm not sure He believes in me anymore."

Then she turns the dial again. There's nothing but static.

Chapter 17

It's the voices of angels, Leon thinks.

"Drive on children, Drive on!" they sing in a deep southern gospel growl. "I'm not worried about my parking space, I just want to see the Savior face-to-face."

There are so many voices it is overwhelming—a cacophony of four-part harmony. Clapping hands keep the beat. "Amens" stretch out like stray cats. The song shakes with thunder and forgiveness.

"Drive on children, Drive on!"

It is the day after Christmas. Sunday. A dishwater cold morning. The cement slab underneath Leon's head hums. For a couple of hours, he's been passed out next to the central air-conditioning unit behind what used to be The International House of Pancakes, just outside of the town of Flamingo. It is the mosquito capital of the world. His body looks like a pincushion. Sweating sour, he places his left ear against the humming unit.

That's where they are, he thinks. The angels. They are inside of the air conditioner.

When the propane blew, Leon's brain shook like an Etch A Sketch. So the idea of angels living in air conditioners seems entirely reasonable at this moment.

They must be real tiny, he thinks, and peers into the metal honeycomb filter to catch a glimpse of them, but all he can see is lint and an M&M wrapper that has worked its way into the metal casing. The Frigid King smells of french fries and maple syrup. Makes his stomach growl. Fire ants crawl in a straight line across his legs. He doesn't notice. He wants to clap along to the music, but his arm is numb—mostly because he's lying on it.

The voices of the angels grow louder. A sax and bass drive them on. "Sing it," Leon shouts.

And they do.

"When you get on the road to glory, Satan is going to try to flag you down. But keep on driving if you want to make it to the holy ground."

Sweet as a dozen of Krispy Kremes, Leon thinks. Not just any dozen. Not glazed, or chocolate, but filled with pure white sweet cream filling and powered sugar all over the top.

Leon leans in even closer. His limp arm hits the metal casing of the Frigid King. The pain is electric, takes his breath away.

"You got to check your tires," the angels in the air conditioner sing. "You got a rough road ahead."

Tears well in Leon's eyes. Cool his fever. "Amen," he says. "Amen."

Leon has crawled all night to arrive behind the IHOP. His world is a kaleidoscope. Words and images rattle around, aimless in his brain. The only thing he is sure of is that he recently met Jesus, and that a choir of tiny angels is singing inside the Frigid King. And they're singing for him.

"That Jesus has got some pull," he says. Then sings along, "Drive on children. Drive on."

He is off-key and croaking. But even through his confusion, Leon knows he is lucky to be alive.

When the explosion happened, he was rolling away from his trailer. That saved him. The force propelled him into the sandy ground near the swamp. When Mayor Bender and the rest arrived with their garden hoses and boxes of baking soda, Leon had rolled into the cattails and was covered in mud. Looked more like a gator than a recreational vehicle salesman.

Drunk and stunned, he slipped in and out of consciousness as his trailer burned.

"He's got to be dead," Leon heard a chalkboard screechy-voiced woman say. For some reason, the sound of her voice made him want to hit her with a spitball.

"Poor son of a bitch," he heard Bender say. Then the mayor impersonated a Doberman barking. A few snarls. Couple of growls.

"Pretty good," Leon thought, then passed out again.

When he finally came to, everything was gone, including, most regrettably, Clyde, who looked about as much like Elvis in his pre–Las Vegas years than any dead bear had a right to, and his 1963 Sovereign of the Road Airstream complete with Sky Dome and extended cab, and his best cowboy boots. The air was filled with the dark scent of scorched metal and burnt tapioca—a smell that brought tears to his eyes, but he didn't know why.

In fact, when he came to, Leon wasn't sure about much. One by one, memories of his life rose to the surface, and then faded. Mama Po in her cheesecake swimsuit cooing over Miss Pearl. Grammy Lettie teaching him how to count cards in poker, "You got to have a skill, boy." Dagmar at Po's funeral, honey-tanned, her hand clammy in his. And Cal, his small fish of a body, bobbing in the rough current.

All this was part of him, and somewhere deep inside he knew it, but didn't want it anymore. Couldn't bear it. So, bit by bit, Leon let go of his past until he was adrift in the body of himself without anchor.

For a long time, he made his way though the swamp. Wild Turkey dulled most of the pain, but his head hurt right through the drunk. He could feel his brain push against bone.

"Settle down," he said. "Just settle down."

The moon shone clay red, made him squint. At dawn, a flock of red ibises banked a turn overhead. Their sanguine wings combined with the sun and filled the sky with flames.

"I could really use some BBQ," he thought and slowly, very slowly, with the blanket still tied around his waist, began to crawl toward what he thought was the highway. There's always a barbecue place near the highway. That is the only thing he knew for sure.

"Maybe they'll even have coleslaw with tiny bits of apple. Fried okra. Jo-Jos with Tabasco. Peach pie with lard crust."

So he crawled along the tangle of swamp and shore. Past the hibernating alligators, softly barking, dreaming of small dogs and wayward children. Past the pig frogs and their squawking duets. Past a cottonmouth sliding down the trunk of a fallen cypress, slipping into the dark water. Past a turkey vulture, its flaming red head, a pompadour.

"Nice hair," Leon said.

The vulture hissed and flew away.

That's when Leon saw the blue roof of the former IHOP and began to think of biscuits with gravy, pancakes with sausages tucked inside. But he only made it as far as the back door before he passed out.

"Keep on driving," the angels in the air conditioner now sing.

"Amen," Leon shouts, and his brain feels as if it could crush ice at any speed, stir, shake, puree, and liquefy.

Inside what was once an International House of

Pancakes, the Sunday service of the Church of the Resurrection has cranked up the volume. Deacon Henry Love pulls the corners of his vest down hard.

"Jesus has gone missing," he booms. The moon of his belly forces the vest to pop up again like toast. "Jesus has gone missing in a world of parking lots and fancy cars."

Leon looks under the ragged fence. Sees tires everywhere. Some with wire wheels, some with gold-plated hubcaps. Logic spins like a silver ball on a roulette wheel. "I'm in a parking lot," he shouts. "There are fancy cars, but Jesus isn't here."

The sax slips alongside a sultry bass line. The IHOP is steamy. Deacon Love vibrates like lead crystal. "Jesus is lost in a parking lot filled with fancy cars and nobody can find him."

"But nobody's looking!" Leon wails into the air conditioner, and then pulls himself up onto his knees. "I'm the only one out here!" He sees that the parking lot is filled with cars, mostly Cadillac and Buick. Long boats of chrome, glinting. A motor city ocean.

"Where are you, Jesus?" Deacon Love cries out into the microphone and rattles the windows, the doors, and the cement slab that Leon is kneeling on.

"Where are you?" the congregation joins in.

The sound is so overwhelming, it occurs to Leon that the angels might not be in the air conditioner, but in the IHOP. Inside. It only makes sense. IHOP offers pancakes from all over the world—and that's some kind of heaven.

Leon is a hungry man, so he steadies himself against the

Frigid King, takes a deep breath, and, with all his strength, makes his way toward the front door of the IHOP and the manager he knows for certain will be standing there in a matching tie and suspenders, holding a menu, ready to seat him with the heavenly choir and pour him a cup of joe, ink black, no cream.

If this is heaven, he thinks, I probably shouldn't ask for the smoking section.

Inside the IHOP, all heaven is breaking loose. Mabel Love, the deacon's wife, is wearing her best dress, a leopard skin print with matching pillbox, and speaking in tongues, the riffs of Babel. Her mother-in-law clogs along to music that only she can hear, her scarecrow arms flailing.

Everyone is on his or her feet feeling Jesus like a cold finger run along the spine.

Leon watches. Amazed. There are angels in high heels and angels in three-piece suits and angels spinning around in circles and angels falling to the ground. There are angels laughing, singing, shouting, and fanning themselves with paper fans provided by the First National Bank and Trust. There are angels everywhere and they are more beautiful than Leon ever imagined them to be.

And they sweat. A lot.

"Dang cool," he says.

"Shh," says Rae Dawn. Six years old, brown-eyed, and fussy, Rae Dawn is sitting on the blue bench where the customers once waited to be seated. The bench is now known as the "time-out place." Rae Dawn sits there so often Deacon Love has threatened to have her name inscribed over it.

Rae Dawn is not an angel. The sight of Leon bruised, bleeding, dressed in a sheet, and crawling toward her on his hands and knees does not frighten her.

"Wanna see my new doll?" she whispers. "My mommy says it cost a lot of money."

Deacon Love and his congregation do not notice Leon stagger in. They are enraptured.

"Let us take a moment to think of this," Deacon Love says, speaks in a loud stage whisper. "Let us take a moment to think of the Son of God lost in a world filled with greed and hatred and longing."

A spotlight snaps on. His hair shines like chrome.

"Let us close our eyes and dwell on this sad vision of our sweet Savior. Let us ruminate. Let us conjugate its meaning."

Deacon Love puts a meaty hand over his eyes. Then everyone, except for Rae Dawn and Leon, puts a hand over his or her eyes.

It looks like they are all playing hide-and-seek. The music stops. The room is suddenly quiet.

"Want a peppermint?" Rae Dawn whispers loudly to Leon, who in an attempt to stand, is teetering back and forth, white knuckled, clutching the doorjamb. She opens her tiny black patent purse.

Over the griddle Leon sees a sign—"If it isn't perfect, send it back."

Got to be heaven's motto, he thinks.

Rae Dawn holds the peppermint out for him. It's fluffy like a tiny pillow. The sweet smell makes his stomach turn.

Then Deacon Love begins to sing, "Swing low, sweet chariot."

The congregation joins in. "Coming for to carry me home."

"Swing low."

The song is soft as sheets. Leon is so tired he wants to curl into it. Let it cover him. Soothe him. Over the sweet rumble of voices, the keyboard softly pulls the melody along. The sax and bass whisper.

"Aren't you gonna eat it?" Rae Dawn says, tugs at Leon's blanket.

"Jesus is lost," Deacon Love cries out over the song. "That we know for sure." Tears roll down his face, splash onto his heaving vest.

"No, he isn't," Rae Dawn shouts. "He's right here. I just gave him a peppermint."

The entire congregation turns around.

Leon, peppermint in hand, waves. "Hey there," he says. Flashes a winning smile. Then passes out.

Chapter 18

Sunday morning. The day after Christmas. Early. Jesus is sitting at the kitchen table in pin-striped trousers waiting for the sun to rise.

In front of him he's placed all the knives he could find—paring, chef, and steak. There's also a straightedge from the bathroom, a bowie that Jimmy Ray keeps underneath the sink, and a machete once used to cut back banana trees.

What to choose?

He'd promised Jimmy Ray that he'd sharpen them. "It's the least I can do," he said. "It will give me a sense of purpose."

And it does. Choosing the right "Tool of Salvation," as he likes to think about it, is as important as the act itself. Each tool has a different effect. The machete is heroic and can be wielded like a samurai—which is fun, but a little overdone these days. The bowie is a classic—just a swift upward movement under the rib cage and twist. The straightedge takes some planning; a little sedative is needed to put the victim out so there's no struggle, but it says so much more than other methods.

Life dripping away. Death easing in. Very Blake. Very poetic.

So it's very difficult to choose. Poisons have their place, but they tend to panic the victim, which can be unsightly. He's always wanted to try a bow and arrow. For someone like Jimmy Ray that might be a nice touch. Very mythical, he thinks. The archer is a classic. Romantic, but not maudlin.

Outside, the sun is just rising over the key lime house. There is a chorus of wild parakeets squalling. And, of course, the tumultuous sound of poultry sex. Jesus picks up the knives, one by one, and sharpens each on the whetstone. Tests them on his hand, or forehead, or forearm—tiny slice after tiny slice. He wants to make sure they're perfect. He likes the cold blade against his skin.

When he gets to the machete, he holds it close to his neck for a moment, runs it along the edge of his thin beard. Bristles bend underneath the weight of the blade. He imagines what it would be like to let the knife slip.

Can't be worse than being stuck inside of Jesus, he thinks. But then he thinks of Jimmy Ray and the mess. Where are my manners? But he doesn't move the machete.

He just sits there with it pressed up against his neck, feels it jump in his hand and counts the beat of his heart like a runner doing laps.

It's then that Dagmar—honey hair deflated, eyes red and swollen—opens the back door without knocking.

"What are you doing?"

To say she is alarmed is an understatement.

Jesus pulls Jimmy Ray's Luger from his pants. Waves it around.

"Waiting for oatmeal."

At the sight of a gun waving through the air like a prom queen Dagmar panics. All she can think of is Jimmy Ray. Why did I leave this maniac with Jimmy Ray?

"What have you done with him?" She lunges for the gun. The kitchen chair falls over backward taking Jesus with it. And Dagmar, too. The machete tumbles to the ground, barely misses her foot.

Jimmy Ray comes out of his bedroom to see what the ruckus is all about. Dressed in his purple silk dressing gown, smelling of violet tonic, his hair marcel-waved, he looks like a deposed king. "My, my sis," he says sweetly. "No need to get excited. There's enough oatmeal for every-body."

"The gun—" she says.

"Isn't loaded."

"Oh."

She rolls off Jesus and lies on the floor. Stares at the ceiling. Feels more than a little stupid.

"There's no need for such a fuss," Jesus says and pulls

himself up to his feet. He brushes off his pants and thinks, I just hate it when they make a fuss.

"You got to excuse my Dagmar," Jimmy Ray tells Jesus. "She is fierce. And a little presumptuous." Jimmy Ray clucks at Dagmar; his eyebrow is raised. Then he leans over slowly, painfully, and extends a hand to help her up. "How many times have I told you not to play on the floor?" he says, teasing. "Don't make me ground you."

Dagmar can see from the look on his face that nobody's told Jimmy Ray about Leon. She'd assumed he knew— Trot, or Bender, or the scanners—but it's clear he doesn't. Why didn't I call? It's then she realizes the room is quiet. The scanners are silent. The lights are out. The blue flame on the gas stove hisses. Power must be out, she thinks. Doesn't take his hand.

Jimmy Ray looks concerned. "You okay, sis?"

"I'm fine," she says, shaky. She sits up. Doesn't sound fine at all. She hugs her knees and looks into Jimmy Ray's yellowed eyes. They are watery, weak, worn away by having seen too much of this world. She reaches out and catches his wrist, feels his pulse beating. Misses him already.

"Last night. Leon—" she says.

"The fire?"

She nods.

Jimmy Ray sits down hard on the kitchen chair. Overwhelmed. He doesn't know how to feel. He's known plenty of men like Leon in New Orleans—good-looking, but not too smart. "The worst combination of man put on this earth," he tried to tell Dagmar, but she wouldn't listen. So he tried to be all right with Leon, tried to make his peace. But then Cal died. Jimmy Ray called Cal "The Sun Child" and was teaching him to riff, telling him stories about Professor Longhair and the boys. And it was Leon's fault. Damn Leon.

The anger rises up in him, again—even though it is not Buddha's way. Just human, he tells himself. Still, the anger makes him feel shamed.

Dagmar puts her head on his lap and starts to cry. Heavy heart, he thinks, and runs a hand through her apricot hair. My little girl has a heavy heart.

"Sugar, let me make you some french toast," he says gently. "I'll even cut it into little hearts like you used to like when you were a baby."

"I'm not a baby anymore."

"You are always my baby girl," he says, and there is something different in the way he says the word *baby*. Not a southernism, but the truth. My baby. My daughter. My child.

And she hears it.

The two sit for a moment in the soft light of the kitchen breathing each other's breaths. Jimmy Ray with his old man watered-down eyes. Dagmar with her Egyptian queen gaze.

"You my baby," he whispers. Tears fill his eyes.

Dagmar nods, overwhelmed. Kisses his leathered hand. "Father," she thinks. "Dad," "Pop," "Papa"—but only "Jimmy Ray" still feels right.

"French toast would be good," she says.

"Anything for you, sis."

And that makes her cry again. She reaches into the pocket of her jeans, pulls out a Kleenex. Blows her nose.

Honks like a Canada goose.

"That's not from my side of the family," Jimmy Ray laughs.

Jesus is sniffling, too. He blows his nose on the dishtowel. With Leon out of the way, he can do Jimmy Ray up right, give him the kind of death that only a friend can give—a death that says you care. Surprisingly, Jesus feels a deep sense of caring for the old man. Never felt that way before.

I'm going to give you the Hallmark Card of Death, he thinks, and is completely choked up over the sentiment. Tears run down his cheeks.

"You going soft on me?" Jimmy Ray asks, wipes a tear away from his own face.

Jesus shakes his head. "Tears of joy," he says. "I just remembered I love french toast."

Chapter 19

It's still unclear who opened the window in Leon's room. The nurses claimed the cleaning staff did. The cleaning staff claimed it was the nurses. What is clear, however, was that the window was only open a crack. But then that's really all that was needed. Honeybees are such tiny things. They don't take up much space.

And so the queen bee slipped through the open window, and the others followed. This, in itself, is not uncommon. When colony populations are too high, the queen always moves part of the group to a new harborage. During these swarms they occasionally work their way into buildings; burrow into walls, chew their way through drywall.

They don't usually swarm onto patients, however.

The slurry of tapioca that had dried in Leon's hair drew them in. The bees were hungry, focused, and looking for a place to build a hive. Leon was in a drug-induced coma. It was a perfect match.

And so the walls of Leon's hospital room now hum like a hundred high-voltage wires.

You never want to disturb bees building a hive—that's the first thing Nurse Becker learned about bees in Camp Fire Girls back when she was a girl in South Miami. So she closes the patient's door slowly. Runs.

Underneath the swarm, Leon's body vibrates like a tuning fork. He's dreaming that he's a Las Vegas marquee. Dang cool, he thinks. I hum. Wayne Newton is headlining.

It's been four hours since Leon was airlifted to the hospital. He's already out of ICU because there's just no room—holidays and all—and besides, he's just another Jesus guy without insurance, or ID, or anything. Just a man in a blanket. His brain has stopped swelling, but he's still listed in critical condition because he's running a temperature of 102 degrees. Nobody can seem to bring it down. There's talk he may have some sort of virus, but the results from blood tests are still at the lab. The doctors avoid his room. It's tough to know what to do with a John Doe named Jesus.

Now there are bees involved.

The bees are swarming through his hair, down his neck, his hands, his arms, and legs. They fill the room like a storm cloud, turn day into night. Leon is nearly completely covered. Only his face, pale as a paper plate, shows through the tangle.

The queen with her five eyes watches Leon closely. The guard bees circle them, snap and buzz. The scouts lay down a thin layer of wax on top of Leon's thin cotton blanket and in the crook of his right arm. The room has a south-facing exposure. It is warm and bright. The bees like that. They quickly lay down layer after layer of wax, weaving a honeycomb as they go. The topaz walls smell like rose petals.

This would all be perfectly natural if Leon were a stump.

As the bees build their hive, their cool bodies and the hundreds of wings chill the air, the honey, and Leon, too.

His temperature is now 99.6. And falling.

"All right," Nurse Becker says. She's gathered the staff together in the hallway. "Here's what we're going to do." She's flushed and sweating. There's no time to waste. She tosses bath towels to the nurses and aides.

"Hold these over your head and duck when I run by."

Nurse Becker is a large woman, all thunder and author-ity. "Everybody ready?" she shouts. Nobody is, but they nod anyway.

Down the length of the hall, nurses with towels on their heads hold patients' doors shut. Bill, the security guard, holds the emergency exit open. Bill's a small man and, if it wasn't for the gun, is the kind of man who is easily overlooked. Nurse Becker always makes the effort to be kind to him, to take a moment and talk. She knows what it's like to be outsized, odd, and alone. Instead of a towel, he's wearing a blanket with holes cut out for his eyes. He looks like a Halloween ghost. She doesn't even think to laugh.

"On the count of three," she shouts.

"Ready?" he shouts back.

"Ready!" she says.

Carefully, slowly, Nurse Becker eases open the door to Leon's room. Accidentally, the door locks in place with a loud clank. The sound makes her jump. The room is angry with bees. This better work, she thinks. Tears fill her eyes. Her legs are shaking.

Quickly, she pops open the lid on the orange blossom honey, which she usually has with her tea. The jar is new. The honey smells of summer, its thick heat.

The second thing Nurse Becker learned about bees in Camp Fire Girls is that when they swarm like this it means they're hungry. And when they're hungry they want honey.

The swarm turns. The hum grows louder; you can hear it all the way down the hospital corridor.

"Run," Bill screams.

But Nurse Becker can't. For a moment she's riveted by fear, by the overwhelming sight of hundreds of bees.

"Run, damn it!"

Leon's temperature is now 98.6. Normal. The coma is lifting. He opens his eyes, but the rest of his body is still unresponsive. Bees cover him. His brain waves ripple like pond water, so he isn't afraid. He knows he should be, but he isn't. He thinks of his new poker buddy Jesus, and how it is said that the animals bow down before him—even the lions and bears.

Nothing will hurt me, Leon thinks. I got me pals in high places. So he listens calmly to the song of the swarming, the rhythm in the hum. One note after another builds toward some sort of gospel crescendo.

They're singing for me, he thinks, and is amazed that the size and shape of angels change from one minute to the next.

I could really use a pancake right now. With butter pecan syrup.

Meanwhile, a handful of guard bees spin off and surround Nurse Becker.

Keep still, she tells herself. Very still.

It takes every ounce of her strength to stand perfectly still—not to breathe, not to cry. She keeps her eyes focused on the open jar. Doesn't look at the angry swarm of bees circling around her.

If the queen doesn't move, Nurse Becker knows that the swarm won't budge, and may eventually attack. But as soon as she thinks this it happens. The queen finally dives into the open jar. The tiny bee quivers above the honey, then shoots straight up and spins from side to side in a perfect figure eight.

The Waggle Dance.

It's been so long since Nurse Becker has even thought of the waggle dance, a silly name for such an important event, that it almost makes her smile. Keep still, she thinks.

The waggle dance is the universal sign that there's honey, and it's good honey, and the workers should stop what they're doing and follow the dancing bee to the source.

The queen flutters her iridescent wings. The delicate dance begins.

How beautiful, Nurse Becker thinks. How amazing these creatures are. She is mesmerized. The guard bees join in. Golden and quick, they swoop and spin around the tiny queen. It is all so elegant. Each movement has such ease that Nurse Becker wonders what it would be like to be so graceful, not to lumber through life.

Then, suddenly the rest of the swarm—waves and waves of hungry bees—scream toward her.

"Get the hell out of there!" Bill shouts. "What are you waiting for?"

His voice slaps Nurse Becker back into the moment.

"Duck," she shouts and runs as fast as she can down the hall. The bees are faster. They begin to overtake her, cover her with a cloud of dust and hum.

The third thing Nurse Becker learned about honeybees is that they can fly faster than you can run, but she just couldn't let a patient die. Especially one who thinks he's Jesus.

"You never know," she'd told Bill. "They can't all be whack jobs."

Nurse Becker is quickly becoming overcome.

"Toss the jar," Bill screams. "Just toss it outside the door."

Bees are stinging Nurse Becker's face and eyes. With all the strength she can muster, she throws the jar of honey out the Emergency Exit door. The bees follow the jar. Swarm over it. Bill slams the door. Nurse Becker's deflates into a heap. Her face is swollen. Her eyes are shut. She can hardly breathe.

"Where's that damn adrenaline?" Bill is shouting.

"I certainly hope Jesus appreciates this," she whispers.

Bill takes her hand gently. Kneels beside her like Casper in prayer.

Chapter 20

Underneath Dagmar's apartment, in The Dream Café, the music kicks into high gear, shakes the floorboards. It's Sunday. Noon. First show. The first show is always the cheerleader routine, a real crowd pleaser. Izzy and Cocoa cartwheel onto the dance floor.

"Are you ready for teen spirit?" Izzy shouts. Her white cheerleading skirt is high around her head. Her G-string is red. Red and white are the school colors of Dagmar's old school, St. Jude's.

"Ready now!" Cocoa replies. "Let's play! Okay?"

The crowd shouts, "Okay!" A few hoot.

Izzy and Cocoa are perfect. Surly and spankable. Twins. Ice blond. About a year ago, Dagmar "discovered" them at the Waffle House down the road. They were working double shifts to save up for breast reduction surgery. Izzy was the cook. Cocoa, a reluctant waitress.

It was 3 A.M. and Dagmar was having a very late dinner of pecan waffles and country ham when some drunk loaded the jukebox with a roll of quarters. And that's bad enough at 3 A.M., but then he did the unthinkable—he punched the entire left side of buttons. Button after button, the drunk selected every song on the Waffle House play list—all fourteen of them. He punched them once, and then a second time, and then again, until all his quarters were gone.

"That's for you, Cocoa," he shouted. "So you never forget me."

Then he stumbled out the door.

Izzy spit, and the Waffle House rhapsody, the bane of all employees, began.

The "rhapsody" is an occupational hazard visited upon all who work for the yellow and white. Every Waffle House has one. It's a smattering of songs written for and about the hash joint. It's corporate policy. Fourteen little jukebox placards, yellow as yolks, must always be on the left-hand side of the jukebox. They're hits never heard on any radio. The styles range from jazz to rock and roll to novelty songs with bad rhymes and insidious hooks. The songs on the list change frequently, but some standards remain like "844,739 Ways to Eat a Hamburger at Waffle

House" by Billy Dee Cox, and the rocking "Waffle Doo Wop," by Eddie Middleton.

They drive the staff slowly insane. Customers play them at great risk.

Three songs in, Izzy jumped across the counter, case cutter in hand, just as "Why Would You Eat Grits Anyplace Else?" by Mary Welch Rogers hit the platter. The rousing homage was a college cheer, a fight song. It was deafening.

"Gimme a 'G'!" Mary Ann and her cheerleading backup singers shouted.

"G!" Izzy and Cocoa shouted back. Then Izzy cut the jukebox plug with the case cutter, and Cocoa tossed all fourteen of the Waffle House hits out the front door like Frisbees.

The rest is Adult Entertainment History.

Now, as Izzy and Cocoa cheer on the crowd beneath them, Trot and Dagmar pretend not to notice. Trot sits like a giant on Dagmar's soft floral print couch; his knees are nearly up around his ears. His hands are sweaty, folded. Looks like he's in detention. It's his day off, but he's been up early investigating the explosion. Something about it nags him. The timing seems odd, too odd. A quarter of a million dollar rig shows up on Christmas Day at Leon's and then he's burned up in a fire?

Not even Leon can be that unlucky. And Trot's been a cop long enough to know that there's no such thing as coincidence.

"Sorry if I woke you," he says to Dagmar again.

Dagmar is still standing by the door, unwilling to sit down. She shifts her weight from left to right. "Had to get up anyway."

Trot looks fresh-pressed. His jeans are ironed with a crease. She imagines him starching them in what probably is a tiny neat apartment, while a tiny loaf of bread is baking in one of those machines.

Don't wait for me anymore, she thinks. Please.

The noon sun sheets in through the blinds like rain.

"Want some coffee?" she asks.

He shakes his head. "Don't want to be any trouble. Just wanted to see how you were."

How she is is still half-asleep and wearing an old football jersey of Leon's that she used to wear when they were still married. It's three sizes too large and touches her knees. Looks as if it's swallowed her whole.

"I could make some coffee," she says. She's still holding on to the front doorknob. She's poised as if she's waiting for the starting gun to go off, the rabbit to hit the track.

Don't run, she thinks. He's only trying to be nice.

"You should sit down," he says.

"Coffee is easy," she says, but doesn't move.

"I'll get it," Trot gets up. She doesn't protest, has no energy for it. Trot goes into the galley kitchen. Despite its small size, it's steel with granite countertops. There's a new gas range and side-by-side refrigerator with flat-screen TV.

Naked must pay well, he thinks.

"Coffee beans are in the freezer," she shouts, still standing by the door.

They are. In fact, they're all that's in the freezer. He opens the refrigerator out of curiosity. There's a pint of cream, seven kinds of hot sauce including a XXX habanero, a bowl of eggs that he suspects came from Jimmy Ray's, and a six-pack of Diet Coke.

Trot grinds the beans. Starts the coffee. Then he pulls out a pan and olive oil. He cracks three eggs and mixes in some cream. The noise makes Dagmar curious. She peeks around the corner. "You don't have to do that," she says.

"I do. I'm hungry. Any garlic?"

"Pantry."

He chops the fist of garlic as well as any chef Dagmar's seen. It goes into the eggs, and he adds some dried chives. He takes a whisk and beats it into froth. Dagmar likes to watch men cook. It's been a long time since anyone made her breakfast. Makes her feel comfortable. Trot knew it would; that's what he was going for. He wants to make her comfortable so that they can talk. His face is still a little red from where she slapped him last night. Once was enough. But he needs answers.

So when the olive oil sizzles on the pan he says, "Now, don't get sore, but I ran the plates on that RV at Lucky's. Do you know someone named Rose Levi? From New York? Or her husband, Irv? Leon ever mention them?"

"This is an official visit?"

You jerk, she's thinking. He can hear it in her voice.

"Come on, don't be like that."

But Dagmar is, indeed, going to be like "that." "So you think Leon swindled this Rose Levi out of the RV?"

"I don't think anything yet. I'm just trying to find out what happened."

"Ever think that maybe they traded it in?" Dagmar is scowling. "Lucky's is a business. People come in off the street and buy RVs. That's how it's done."

At Lucky's?

That's what he wants to say, but doesn't. Knows better. Trot can't remember the last time Leon had anything worth buying. He also wants to say that Leon is a gambler—and not a very good one. *Come on, Dagmar, we all know that. He'll do anything for a buck.* But what Trot says is, "I'm sure that's probably what happened. It's just that I have to check up on these things."

In the frying pan, the eggs set into an omelet. The kitchen is fragrant with them. Trot jiggles the pan, pays attention to the eggs. He can feel Dagmar's anger, doesn't want to meet her eye.

"So what *aren't* you telling me?" she says.

He hesitates, and then says, "A lot." He shakes the pan a little too hard; the cooked eggs fall away from the sides. "It's an open investigation."

And it is. And all he has is questions. At 4:30 A.M., Trot made a quick check on the Internet and discovered that the American Dream RV is worth more cash than Leon has probably ever seen in his life. But there didn't seem to be any paperwork at the Round-Up about it. Or keys. Trot suspects that Leon had them with him when the explosion occurred. And what about that woman Trot and Carlotta saw Leon talking to at 2 A.M.? Rose Levi?

If so, what would a seventy-eight-year-old nearly blind woman be doing at that hour with Leon? And where was her husband?

The Levis seem to be the key to this case, but no one knows where they are. When Trot called their home number in New York, he was routed to Miami. Nobody answered. So he used a cross directory and called a neighbor back in Cicero. After some convincing, the suspicious Mrs. Edda Miller told him two things of interest.

First, the Levis were going to Florida—"To die," as Rose apparently told Mrs. Miller—"where everybody else is dying." Not exactly a Chamber of Commerce motto, but more than accurate. And the second thing Mrs. Miller said was that the Levis had no children.

"Just the two of them. I half expected you to tell me that they did one of those murder-suicide pacts. They were married for sixty-one years. Wouldn't surprise me."

Nor Trot. But how did Leon fit in? Mrs. Miller didn't have a clue. "This Leon lived in Whale Inlet, you say? Where is Whale Inlet?"

"Harbor," Trot corrected. "Whale Harbor."

"Inlet. Harbor. Who cares?"

I do, Trot thought, and thanked Mrs. Miller for her time. He seemed to be getting nowhere fast.

"You hungry?" he asks Dagmar. She nods, seems a little less angry. He turns the perfect omelet onto a plate, and the coffeemaker beeps. Dagmar serves the coffee. Trot divides the eggs. The moment has turned comfortable again, domestic. He sits down and takes off his baseball cap. He is waiting for Dagmar to pick up her fork, so that they can eat.

Manners, she thinks. His mother trained him well.

Dagmar takes the XXX habanero sauce from the refrigerator and splashes it on her plate until the egg looks as if it's been bludgeoned. Trot's eyes are watering from the fumes.

She shakes the bottle at him. "What some?"

"No thanks," he coughs. "Makes my head sweat." He pats his thinning hair. "Not a pretty sight."

She sprinkles a few drops on his eggs, anyway. "Good for your heart," she says. "Besides, I've seen your sweat before."

And it's true. Trot has sweated with Dagmar in backseats, in tents, and once, during the night of their junior prom, in a hammock. He had rope burns for a week. His face turns red at the memory.

They know each other so well that she can feel him think this. "I meant in the summer," she laughs. "I've seen you sweat in the summer." She rolls her eyes. "Stop blushing."

His face goes flush again. "It's the hot sauce." Sweat is now pouring from his head like rain.

"Good?"

He coughs. "Hot."

For a while they eat without speaking. All that can be heard is Cocoa and Izzy in The Café below them. They are stripping away with collegiate vigor. After a while Dagmar says, "You know Leon is really more decent than you give him credit for." And as soon as she says it, she regrets it. Trot stops chewing. Goes pale. She was only trying to explain, but it came out like an accusation.

"He's a decent guy," she tries again. "Really."

"Was," Trot wants to say, "Leon *was* decent," but he doesn't. "He was my best friend," he says quietly. "I did love him." Then Trot puts his fork down.

Dagmar feels his sorrow. No longer hungry, she pushes her plate away.

"Gimme an 'S!'" Izzy and Cocoa shout beneath them in unison.

"S!" The crowd shouts back. Enthusiastic.

Trot folds his napkin and places it next to the coffee cup. "I should go. Sorry about the mess in the kitchen."

"Look, I'm sorry—"

Trot nods. It's clear that they are both missing Leon. Despite everything—all the history, all the pain—they miss him.

Beneath them the dancers work the crowd.

"Gimme an 'E'!"

"E!" the crowd responds.

"Gimme an 'X'!"

"X!"

"Gimme an S! Gimme an E! Gimme an X!"

Izzy and Cocoa bounce in unison. "Whadda ya got?" They lift up their tiny pleated skirts. The crowd hoots and whistles.

"SEX!"

The word is thunderous.

Trot can smell sleep on Dagmar's skin: like baby powder, like silk. His face feels so hot he thinks he can grill on it. "I really just stopped by because I thought you might need something," he says. It nearly feels true.

Downstairs the crowd kicks into a boozy version of "On Wisconsin." Pom-poms fly.

"So, do you need anything?" he asks.

Dagmar shrugs.

The crowd sings, "Fight, fellows, fight, fight, fight! We'll win tonight!"

The floorboards underneath Trot and Dagmar's feet shake. It's difficult to ignore any longer.

Trot winces. Dagmar looks closely at him. For the first time, she actually sees him for who he is now, not who he was back then, so long ago. The years have changed him, as they've changed her. They've deepened the lines around his mouth. He's thinner now. Hard-edged. Filled with more sorrow than she remembers.

"I should go then," he says. Stands.

"Sure."

He's standing so close, she can feel the heat of his skin, smell the peppermint Life Saver.

She leans against his chest, exhausted.

Trot puts his arms around her. He feels tentative. He's unsure if she'll run away from him again. Or slap him. But still he holds her.

"Nobody gets to stay forever," he says simply.

The moment is awkward: a mix of desire, fear, and sorrow. Without a word, she kisses him. At first, the kiss is gentle. Then the wanting takes hold, then the grief.

He pulls her closer. She can feel his heart beat.

Underneath their feet, the crowd yells, "Touchdown!"

"I really have to move," Dagmar softly laughs and touches the side of Trot's face with the back of her hand. He blushes. It's been so long since she's seen him blush. She's forgotten how beautiful his smile is, how gentle.

He kisses her fingers. She closes her eyes. He holds her in his arms, tightly, as if it were for the last time—because it is. He can't do this anymore. Can't love her. It's too painful. Too complicated. Now, there's Carlotta—he can't stop thinking about her even though she may be dead. Her voice like crushed velvet.

As if on cue, Trot's cell phone rings. It's Bender, he's laughing.

"Guess what pretty gal just walked into The Pink?"

Trot doesn't have to guess. He knows.

Beneath his feet, the applause is deafening.

Chapter 21

All Trot knew for sure was that Leon and Carlotta met in Vegas.

She was dealing cards in a small place just off The Strip called The Desert Aire. The Aire had a worn aqua charm with an all-meat buffet. "Fifty kinds of meat!" the sign read. "Bar-B-Que. Boiled Beef. Chipped Beef." All fifty types were listed in alphabetical order. Painted on the wall. That drew Leon in. He's a man who likes his beef, especially for "The one low low price of $6.95!"

Once inside the revolving glass doors of The Desert Aire, Leon knew he'd made the right decision. The place smelled of bleach and gravy, reminded him of Sunday dinner at Mama Po's. Made him feel lucky. Leon hadn't felt lucky in a long time.

When he first saw Carlotta, she was playing solitaire at the poker table. She had no choice. It was 4 A.M. and the place was deserted. In the dim light, she was sequin beautiful. Low cut and longing. "I like a woman who defies gravity," Leon said to her chin-high cleavage. So she dealt him in.

A couple of hands, he thought, then I'll move on to somewhere else.

But once Leon sat down he never left. There was something about Carlotta that he couldn't walk away from. It wasn't so much that she was beautiful—up close she wasn't that beautiful at all—but she listened to him in a way he hadn't been listened to in a long time.

"How'd that make you feel?" she'd say every now and then. She sounded as if she really wanted to know. After a while, Leon found himself talking about all kinds of things he never really talked about with anyone. Carlotta had that way about her. She was easy to talk to and that made him think that he knew her, made him think she was his friend.

By the time sunrise came around, Leon was losing money, winning a little, losing a lot more. It didn't matter. He didn't care. He figured that she knew that. Listening was her job, helped the house win, but he still told her about Grammy Lettie, Pettit's Alligator All-Stars, and his beloved Miss Pearl, "The Amazing One-Ton Wonder."

"'Miss Pearl, you sure are a looker,' I used to say. 'You are my best girl.'"

"Everybody needs a best girl," Carlotta said softly, and it made him wonder if she was anybody's best girl. Or used to be. Or wanted to be.

Then he told her the part of the story he didn't even want to think about. He told her about Miss Pearl and the night he waited with her for the men to come and take her away. How she seemed to know it was over. Her head on his lap. How she looked at him.

"You know," he said, "I still got that straw hat. All these years."

Then Leon coughed. Rubbed his eyes. "That's messed up, isn't it?" he said. "Some kind of messed up."

Carlotta had worked at The Desert Aire for nearly five years. She'd seen a lot of men, heard a lot of stories, took a lot of money—it was her job after all—but there was something about Leon and his love for a toothless alligator that touched her. Something odd, she had to admit, but something sweet. He didn't seem like all the other marks, so she leaned across the blackjack table and wiped the tear from his cheek with her cocktail napkin.

"The cold-blooded ones always break your heart," she whispered. Her hair hung away from her face for a moment.

It was then that Leon could see the scar clearly. He figured it wasn't an accident, made him feel sad for her. So he kissed her. At first, it was out of pity. But by the time he kissed the scar all the way down her hairline, Leon found himself kissing her because he wanted to. He was kissing her because of the steel inside her—the knowing how life can sometimes turn on you, but you have to keep going, can't give up—that kind of steel. He liked that in a woman. Didn't see it often. So he kissed her until the security guards escorted them both out of the casino. He kissed her until they tossed her purse out into the street.

But, three weeks later, Leon and Carlotta were all razors and elbows. Leon figured it had something to do with the lack of large oceangoing mammals in Whale Harbor.

"The longing for large aquatic life is a powerful force," Grandma Lettie once told him. "Not an easy thing to get over." Now he understood.

Had Trot known all this, the real details of Carlotta and Leon's life together, he might have stopped by Pettit's All-Star Alligator Farm, or what's left of it, just to take a look. He might have suspected that she was there waiting for Leon in the one place that brought them together. She was there waiting to start a new life.

But Trot didn't know any of that. Didn't even suspect it. How could he? Nobody had been to Lettie Pettit's in a long time, over twenty years. There was no reason to go. The former alligator farm sat at the edge of town, on a peninsula, where the Gulf of Mexico meets the harbor. Nobody lived out that far anymore. Over time the road had become overgrown by passion fruit vines, deep red and purple. They crosshatched the canopy of live oaks, knit them together like fingers. They make the road impossible to drive though especially in spring when thousands of monarch butterflies come to rest, their burnished wings beating.

And no one would come by boat. The shore around Lettie's house had always been too shallow. Sandbars and swift currents hugged the coast.

At least, that's the way it used to be.

During the past forty years, currents have eroded the shoreline and caused the sand to shift. Now, at that point in the harbor, there's a bayou with a thriving ecosystem. Manatees breed freely. Shrimp swim in the fists of mangrove roots. Mullets and grouper churn the waters.

And, perhaps more surprisingly, the sand around Lettie's house has eroded. The house, with its rusted tin roof, has risen. The four walls, the front stairs—it's all there.

It's not really a miracle, although it appears to be one. The house was built in the early 1920s; constructed tongue and groove from "junk wood"—cypress trees that were cleared to put in the roads.

Cypress is an amazing wood. Ancient Egyptians used it for their mummy cases. Medieval craftsmen carved it into cathedral doors. It is naturally decay and insect resistant. It was once used for water tanks, water troughs, and well casings. It has little tendency to warp, twist, or cup. It will last forever.

But in 1920, in Whale Harbor, nobody knew that. All they knew was that it was free.

And so, all these years later, the tiny cypress house stands again, level as the day it was built. Saltwater and sun have bleached it into driftwood, reedy as knees, and the tin roof looks more like a rusted doily than a roof, but the walls stand. And only a few windows are broken. It looks, more or less, just as Mama Po and Grammy Lettie had left it. The curtains, now shredded and gray, still hang in the windows. Underneath, flower boxes seem ready to be planted. The white picket fence is peeling and rotted in most places. But the entrance gate, a gate like no other with its gigantic gator grin, is only slightly diminished. It leans a little more to the right than usual, but it still stands. Its pointy teeth appeared decayed. Its faux-gator skin is bleached to a pastel shade of green. But its sign, "You pays your money, you takes your chances," still hangs and is still legible. Still provides fair warning.

"It's not so bad," Carlotta said when she first saw the place. She rolled up the sleeves of her old gray sweatshirt, adjusted the crown of red and purple passion fruit flowers that she'd made from the vines, and carried her suitcase up the walk. She never expected the house to still be here. She really thought that all she'd find was a gate and an old ticket booth.

But here it was: Grandma Lettie's. The moment felt like Christmas was supposed to feel—magical and kind. The house felt like a gift. Its bleached silver driftwood shone. The shaded porch was hairy with algae, but the front door was open and she took it as a good sign.

"All this needs is a little bleach."

Luckily, there was still a bottle under the kitchen sink.

Chapter 22

Early the next morning a crowd of patients came to see the man who was known as "Bee-Jesus." They lined up outside of Leon's door in wheelchairs, some with IVs hanging from poles. Some were on oxygen; hoses lay across their bellies like snakes sunning themselves.

Bill, the security guard, was called in for crowd control.

"Good thing you called me," he told Nurse Becker who was still recovering from the bee stings; looked plucked like a fat goose. "You never know when a mob can turn."

"They're in wheelchairs," she told him. "Some of them can't even walk."

He gave a grave look, pulled up his pants.

"Just keep them out of the room until I finish my morning coffee," she said.

After the bee incident, Nurse Becker had refused to go home. The hospital was critically understaffed during the holiday season. They needed her and she liked to be needed.

"Can I bring you back coffee?" she asked Bill.

"Just take care of yourself," he said gently.

"If you can get them back into their rooms, that would be good."

"I'll do my best."

"You always do."

The thought that Nurse Becker saw him as a competent man inspired Bill. As soon as she entered the break room, he pulled out his gun.

"All right, everybody, listen up."

His voice rattled the breakfast trays that lined the hallway waiting for sunrise. "This is a restricted area."

And then he told the story of how he saved Bee-Jesus from the swarm of killer bees. He didn't really mean to tell the story that way, leaving out Nurse Becker's heroic act, but since he had everyone's attention, and that didn't happen often, and he did have a gun in his hand, as all good heroes often do, the story just came out that way.

"They were African bees," Bill said sagely, his voice was nearly a whisper. "Killers."

He said this with such conviction that even he believed it. And, as he wove the stunning story of his heroism, total fabrication that it was, the truth became so fluid, so embellished with such courageous flourish, that even those who saw the mountainous Nurse Becker with honey in hand save the day nearly believed him.

"I kept a cool head," he said, and then aimed his Smith and Wesson at an imaginary swarm of oncoming bees. At that moment, he looked a lot like a tiny John Wayne impersonator at the shooting gallery of the Florida State Fair. "BAM! BAM! BAM!" Bill said over and over again. Quarter after quarter. No stuffed flamingos.

And when every last imaginary bee had been blown away Bill said ominously, "I tell you this story because I can't guarantee the bees aren't still around. They could be lurking in the shadows just waiting to finish this poor slob off.

"These are wily bees."

Then Bill "buzzed."

He buzzed, long, loud, and hard. He buzzed as if he himself were a hive of killer African bees. It was an odd, thin, unerringly unnerving sound. His cheeks turned fat as goldfish. His face went red. At one point he even closed his eyes, enraptured. Bill wanted to give the crowd a sense of the danger that he had faced, a sense of urgency, and a true understanding of his newly imagined bravery.

However, he just ended up spitting on most of them until they wheeled away.

When Nurse Becker came back from her coffee break, she was impressed that the corridor was empty. "I'll take it from here," she said.

"I don't think they'll be coming back." Bill patted his Smith and Wesson and gave her a "John Wayne" nod. "When I disperse a mob, they stay dispersed."

Nurse Becker didn't laugh. She never laughed at Bill. They were both odd-sized people who knew what it was like to dream odd-sized dreams. "Thanks," she said kindly, and meant it. "I'm sure they won't be back."

"They won't."

Bill was wrong. Once breakfast was served, one by one, they came back. They lined their wheelchairs up outside of Leon's door. They wanted to see him. Wanted to pat his head for luck. Wanted to believe in Bee-Jesus.

Leon, however, wanted to sleep.

"I don't understand why they're out there," he whined to Nurse Becker. "I know Jesus and I'm not him."

"Glad to hear it," she said. "I know him, too, and accept him as my personal savior."

"Has he ever taken you for a ride in his dang cool RV?"

She added a bit more Valium to Leon's IV drip. "Sweet dreams," she said.

Ever since the fever left, it's been this way. Leon would remember something about his life, and Nurse Becker would tell him that the doctors don't want him to strain his brain too much.

"Darling, you've had quite a shock."

"But I'm a Round-Up Cowboy," he said. "Bob the Round-Up Cowboy. I rope them in."

"Uh huh."

Nurse Becker often made very long notes on Leon's chart.

For example, after Leon's postbreakfast nap it became clear to him that he was an heir to the throne of some small country. So he buzzed her.

"It just makes sense," he explained. "I can't stop dreaming of kings and queens."

"They'll be plenty of time to figure that out later, sugar," she said, and added a tiny bit more Valium to his IV. "You have to rest your brain for now. Just sleep."

Sleep is good, Leon thought. The drugs made him sleep in the most amazing way. It was a deep gentle sleep with vivid dreams in which he invents ways to fly without airplanes, or makes friends with tall brown bears who wear sunglasses and have a striking resemblance to Elvis in his pre–Las Vegas years.

Dang cool.

After a while, it became clear to Leon that whoever he was before his brain got shook, he's pretty sure that he was the kind of man who needs plenty of sleep. The kind who needs to dream dreams big enough for an entire nation— hopefully one in a tropical climate.

But people kept sneaking in.

"Hey! Wake up, Miracle Guy!" said Sam. He was the first one who made it past Nurse Becker. There was a bedpan incident in Room 201, lots of screaming and chaos, so Sam made a break for it. Rolled right in while nobody was looking.

Sam was twenty years old, a bleached-blond mountain of a boy. Also known as "Gator Boy." This is not because of his school affiliation, although he'd been a freshman at the University of Florida for over three years, but because when he was sixteen years old he sucker punched a gator who tried to make him lunch. The gator was fifteen feet long and hiding under Sam's foster parents' pickup—which was inconvenient because Sam was trying to steal it at the time.

The gator lurched at the punch. Sam lost an ear, but KO'd the reptile. A tabloid reporter picked up the story and renamed him "Gator Boy." And it stuck. He used to be known as "Bubba."

Sam was a young man ardently confident in his own abilities. He had a likeness of his own face tattooed on his arm with the phrase "In $am We Trust" underneath it—which is a lot snappier than "In Gator Boy We Trust." He also pointed out to Leon that the "S" in his name had been replaced by a dollar sign. "Cool, huh? That's because I'm worth my weight in gold. Coach said."

Leon, floating on a tranquilized cloud, waved down at Sam and smiled like the deposed prince he knew he was. Said nothing.

Sam is what Nurse Becker calls a hard case. Had a football scholarship from Gainesville, and a high-powered sports agent, until, drunk in Miami, he lost his leg in a motorcycle accident on Thanksgiving Day. It happened right after the bowl game. He killed the girl he was riding with.

"She was just a fan," Sam told the press.

A month later, all his fans are gone and his agent won't return his calls. But Sam keeps thinking he's going to play again, even though the doctors haven't even fit him with a leg that he can successfully walk with, let alone run. He's just so big he's nearly impossible to fit. They will have to have a prosthesis specially made, but Sam has no insurance, and no donor is willing to step forward. His family abandoned him long ago. The comment about the girl did not endear him to the public. So hospital administration is trying to find someone willing to donate a wheelchair so Sam can be released. After that, he's on his own.

"I'm star potential," he told Leon when they first met. "Always been a star. It's only natural that I'd be the first NFL player in history with only one leg. The draft is coming up in a couple of months. If I'm in, I'll see that you're taken care of. I'll be rich. You'll be rich, too."

Nurse Becker arrived before Leon could answer.

"Sam, we got to get you back," she said and started to wheel the boy away.

"Wait!" Sam panicked, grabbed Leon's hand. "Look, man," he said, "if you could just get my agent to call me back." Then he placed his football letter jacket at the foot of Leon's bed. "Kind of a down payment." When he said this, he sounded a little less cocky. "If you fix it for me, that jacket will be worth something someday. I'll be the first one-legged player in the NFL. When I win the Super Bowl you can sell it on eBay and retire."

Nurse Becker picked up the jacket and put it back on the young man's lap. She knew it wouldn't help Sam to tell him that there was no miracle. This Bee-Jesus is just another crazy fella in a sheet. Another whack job.

"Sugar," she said gently. "While Jesus appreciates the gesture, being who he is he could not possibly wear a

Florida Gators jacket. Would that be fair to all those good Christian boys and girls at Florida State University? Or Miami International?"

Sam thought about the logic of this. "Oh," he said. "Makes sense."

She knew it would. That's why Nurse Becker is Nurse Becker.

When she rolled Sam out into the hallway she told the crowd, "You all should just go back to your rooms. There's not much to see." And she sounded sad. She hoped, at least a little, that this Jesus was different from all the rest. It was Christmas, after all.

During that first day, Bee-Jesus spent a lot of time sleeping. Every now and then, he'd cry out as if speaking in tongues. "The river card! Fourth street! Alligator blood! All in! Go all in!"

He seemed to be troubled in a way Nurse Becker had never seen before. Before she went home, she kissed the sleeping Leon on his forehead. "Good night, sweet prince," she said. She couldn't help herself. He seemed like a little boy lost in his imagination. "I hope your kingdom is warm and always sunny."

"Dang cool," he mumbled and fell into a flying dream.

About 2 A.M. Sam came back. "Hey, Miracle Guy," he said and shook Leon by the arm until he was awake.

Leon opened his eyes. Sam looked tired. "Can I at least rub your head for luck?" he asked.

There was something about the lumbering boy that reminded Leon of a real alligator—the sad look in his eyes, a knowing—but Leon couldn't imagine where he'd gotten that idea. He was pretty sure he'd never met a real alligator, especially one this large. They don't seem to be that social a creature, he thought, too many teeth. But for some strange reason Leon felt affection for Gator Boy, although he had a disturbing urge to put a straw hat on him and ask him to say "Howdy."

"I'll be bigger than William the Refrigerator Perry," Sam told Leon. "You just got to get my agent to call me back."

Leon, his eyes as wide as hamburgers, just nodded.

The next morning, the believers came again. It was Bill's day off, so crowd control was difficult. Outside his room, Leon could hear Nurse Becker tell the story of the bees.

"They had begun the waggle dance," she'd say with such authority that those who have never been a Camp Fire girl knew the phrase meant something, something miraculous. Since the hospital was so understaffed, Nurse Becker was often called away. And so, one by one, the faithful wheeled themselves into Leon's room, told their story, asked for a miracle.

Every time this happened, Leon learned one more thing that he really didn't want to know.

"Do you know how long a man can live without a liver?"

Leon did know, and so he was planning to tell Nurse Becker that this couldn't go on any longer. He was tired of being Bee-Jesus: the Miracle Guy.

But then the miracle happened.

An old Mexican nun saw it first. Sister Inez Alverez came to the hospital for gallbladder surgery. "Four slits in your belly, and we'll yank that sucker out," the doctor told her. He was speaking loudly, because he assumed the old nun knew very little English. "Have you back in 'Ave Maria Land' in no time flat. Zip. Zip." Then he grinned at her with his perfectly veneered teeth.

"Zip. Zip?" she asked, incredulous.

"Zip. Zip," he shouted.

Had Sister Inez Alverez not taken an oath of humility, at that very moment she would have told the doctor that before she became a nun she was a medical exchange student and did her residency at Johns Hopkins.

Probably the year you were born, Gringo.

She knew Americans liked the word *gringo* because they used it in all their westerns.

Still, that would have been wrong to say. Spiteful. Prideful. Fun, but wrong.

So she said. "Bless you, Me-stir Doc-ter!" And she spoke loudly, smiled that "I-Got-Me-A-Burro-So-I-Am-Happy" kind of smile that she'd seen in *The Treasure of Sierra Madre*, a movie that long ago she had decided not to hold against director John Huston because she liked *Amazon Queen* so very much.

Then she said a prayer for the doctor. And two for herself.

Still, it was true. Zip. Zip. A laser, a hose, a digital camera in her belly—and ten minutes later, she was a new woman. Medical science had come a long way since her days as a resident. The surgery was quite simple. The painkillers, divine. And while she wasn't exactly feeling all that well—sliced up and sans gallbladder—since Jesus was around, Sister Inez Alverez, operating under a delicious Vicodin cloud, thought it was just professional courtesy to pay her respects. Especially since she was still feeling a little guilty about the doctor incident, and the fact that while under sedation she fantasized about grinding his store-bought tan body into taco meat and feeding it to a pack of wild miniature Chihuahuas.

"How's that for a stereotype?" she kept on screaming. "We don't need no stinking badges!"

She had to scream to be heard over the mariachi band.

Anger issues—just one of the many reasons Sister Inez Alverez had joined the Carmelites.

"Holy Mother of God!" she screamed when she entered Leon's room.

An overactive imagination was the other.

Nurse Becker ran down the hall, threw the door open, half-expecting more bees. But there, in the fading light of day, was the Virgin Mary's image on Leon's window. It was the very same window through which the swarm of bees had entered. It was just a trick of the light, the sun setting through streaky glass. But the Virgin was smiling and waving a "Hey there!" kind of wave. So it was all rather convincing.

"Dude!" Sam the Gator said.

Leon could see it, too. It nearly scared the Bee-Jesus out of him.

And so the wire services picked up the story. And Sam the Gator called Harlan Oakley, the tabloid reporter who first called him "Gator Boy."

Sam might not know enough to ever become a junior at Florida State University, but he knows a reporter who will pay for a somewhat accurate eyewitness account when he sees one. And, if this guy really is a Miracle Guy, Sam thinks, even better.

Chapter 23

The ghost house has risen, Trot thinks as he walks through the gigantic gator grin and opens the gate that after all these years still nearly shuts tight. He's never seen anything like this house before. Bleached to the bone, it sits in what seems to be a crater. The Gulf of Mexico rolls around the sides of it and back again.

It's low tide, he thinks. Winter. Could be only a matter of months before the entire house will be pulled into the ocean. But of course, it took forty years to whittle away the sinkhole, so you never know. Could take forty more. Or a good storm. Or, maybe not.

He knocks on the door. The smell of bleach is over-whelming.

"It's open!"

It's Carlotta's voice, but she sounds all business. Doesn't remind him of crushed velvet, or prom night. Just sounds like somebody who is in the middle of something and doesn't want to be bothered.

"Miss Carlotta?"

He opens the door and it's 1960 all over again. The television is nearly as big as a porch swing but has a tiny round screen. There's a set of TV tables rusted in a stand by the window and a cocktail table in the shape of a kidney. The small couch has plastic covers to protect its cushions. Reminds Trot of his mother's couch. "You going to put the couch in the freezer, Ma?" he always says to her when he visits. Teases her about living a Ziploc life.

Now he will never tease her again. The wooden frame of the couch is rotted in most places, but the cushions look nearly new.

Trot wonders what else his mother is right about. Probably everything, he thinks. Gives him the willies.

"Miss Carlotta?" he says again. He's nervous. Not sure why he's so nervous, but when Carlotta walks out of the kitchen it becomes clear. He just needed to see her again. Just wanted to make sure she was really alive, really that beautiful.

And she is. Without a doubt. At least to him.

Outside the ghost house, a cloud moves away from the sun and the room is suddenly filled with light. Everything looks silver. Shines. Takes his breath away. Or maybe it's the bleach. Or maybe Carlotta. It's hard to tell. His eyes are watering profusely.

She is so beautiful, he thinks over and over again.

Carlotta is wearing cutoffs and a T-shirt with so many holes it looks as if it's made of Swiss cheese. She holds the bleach-soaked mop like a scepter. There's a fresh crown of passion fruit flowers in her hair. Her pink rubber gloves glow. Her scar is not hidden. In the silvery light it looks more like delicate lace edging her face. Makes her seem even more beautiful.

Trot is speechless.

"Nice to see you, Sheriff," she says, sweetly. Seems to be blushing a little. At least, that's what Trot hopes.

He nods. Clears his throat. His mind is blank.

"You okay?" she asks.

He nods again. Then, like a newborn, he coughs until he is red-faced. Carlotta suddenly looks alarmed. When he finally catches his breath, "Miss Carlotta," he says in a voice that he remembers from puberty: two octaves higher than his own, and splintered.

Not exactly the sort of effect he was going for.

Carlotta puts a bleached arm around him. "You sure you're okay?"

Trot shakes his head, but before he can say anything else, the smell of bleach overwhelms him. Burns in his throat. He starts to cough again. At first, it's just a tickle. Then it seems as if his lung is about to eject itself.

Get a grip, he thinks, sweating. This is unprofessional. This is not going well. But Carlotta looks exceedingly concerned, and he likes that.

"I got some water, hang on," she says and goes into the kitchen. Comes back out with a half-filled bottle in her hand. "I only took a couple of sips. I hope that's okay."

Perfect, he thinks.

She wipes the top of the bottle on her T-shirt. Even better.

Trot now, officially, wants to be that shirt.

He takes a long drink from the bottle and coughs a few times. Takes another drink. It's a slow process for Trot to recover from the overdose of her beauty, and the fear it inspires. But when he finally does and finds his voice, he says, "Miss Carlotta, what are you doing here?"

The question makes her go pale. "I was waiting for Leon."

Was.

She shrugs. Wraps her arms around her shoulders. "I heard the explosion, but . . ." Trails off. Looks away.

Trot wants to hold her, but can't. Not professional, he tells himself, and wonders why she stayed out here so long without heat or electricity. But she seems so upset, he's afraid to ask.

Truth is this: she stayed because she's in love.

She heard the explosion. Saw the flash of light. Watched the fire in the distance. Didn't move. Of course, she didn't know it was Leon, but still. She just sat on the cypress porch and watched the stars hang low over the harbor, fat as fruit. Watched the bats as they wove around each other— blind, yet so graceful. Watched the ancient sea turtles lumbered onto shore, uncaring as gods.

At the time of Leon's reported demise, Carlotta was

falling in love with this place, the ghost house—its pounding surf, its warm taffy salt air.

As a family of cats walked along the moonlit shore, Carlotta couldn't imagine ever leaving this place. She'd never been anywhere so wild, and so kind, at the same time. The mother and three kittens were as big as hunting dogs. They had crooked tails, and a cowlick in the middle of their backs. Long Roman noses.

Panthers, she thought, and remembered that Trot said they could eat you. But it didn't seem possible. They looked quite sweet as they whistled back and forth to each other. Made little peeping sounds. Every now and then one of the kittens would veer away from the pack and the mother would pick it up by the nape of its neck and carry it back to the others in her teeth. Lick the top of its head. Whistle and coo. Then they would all move on.

But she doesn't tell Trot any of this. She can't. It seems too personal. Besides, now that Leon is dead, she knows she'll have to leave. The thought pains her. She gets a faraway look in her eyes.

"You okay?" he asks.

She shrugs.

Trot knows he should ask her where she was at the time of the accident—did she hear the explosion—any number of questions that a good sheriff should ask, but he can't. She is just so beautiful—her crown of passion fruit flowers, the delicate lace of her face—and alive.

"Need anything?" he says.

"More bleach."

Chapter 24

It's Happy Hour and the Blind Brothers' Blues Band is playing low down and dirty. Jimmy Ray growls, "Don't send me no doctors cause doctors won't do me no good." His eyes are closed. His body sways. He seems to have crawled into the music. It pulses through him.

The crowd would be his, if there still were a crowd.

Happy Hour at The Dream Café is usually packed. But at this moment, the only customer left in the place is Jesus. He's sitting against the back wall beneath the "Hall of Fame" photos, which include a series of sixteen-by-twenty-four full-color candid shots of "Roxy the Rabbit Girl" and "Naughty Nurse Nanci." Each dancer is captured at the height of her career. Each photo illustrates a set of particular skills.

The range of limberness is breathtaking.

But Jesus isn't looking at the photographs. He's intent on the band. In the dark, his white sheet glows. The ancient black men, their bones rattling the blues, move in and out of songs with great sorrow and real wisdom. Jesus' bare feet are tapping. His head nods along. He whistles with the harmonica. He even got up once and did the hand jive—unfortunately the band was playing "Handyman" at the time.

And so The Café is empty.

Dagmar, perched at the bar, watched the steady flow of customers out the door. She hoped that it would stop on its own. However, when a bachelor party of twenty left before their orders could be taken, she panicked. She grabbed the man she thought was the groom and said, "Hey! He's not Jesus, he's just crazy!"

Unfortunately, the man did not find this comforting. Nor did anyone else. People then began to push as they fled.

That was about the time that Bernie, sounding every inch of Irish Catholic with immigrant parents from County Cork that she is, said, "Dagmar, girls told me to tell you that the show's canceled tonight. They just can't with him out here."

Then she made the sign of the cross.

Bernie's match-red hair was still in hot rollers. She held her worn pink chenille bathrobe at the neck so tightly her knuckles were pale. She looked ready for a slumber party, not a strip show. Jesus was singing along with Jimmy Ray. "She was a red-hot hootchie-cootcher! Hi-de-hi-de-hi-di-hi! Ho-de-ho-de-ho-de-ho!"

"Even Syd the Atheist doesn't want to go out," Bernie said.

Off to the side of the stage, Dagmar could see the cluster of dancers standing in their bathrobes watching Jesus watch Jimmy Ray. Dagmar sighed.

"Happy Hour's nearly over," she told Bernie. "He'll be gone soon."

"So you're telling me that Jesus just came by for free nachos?"

Dagmar frowned. "You do know he's not Jesus, don't you?"

Bernie looked confused. "Well, yeah. Of course. I mean—sure. But he's still leaving, right?"

"Soon as this set's over."

"Good."

"Good."

Bernie hesitated. "It's too bad he's not Jesus, though. That'd be something, wouldn't it?" She sounded wistful.

"Yes," Dagmar said, watching him roll his head around to the beat like Little Stevie Wonder. "That would *really* be something if he was Jesus."

On stage, Jimmy Ray now rumbled on. "If my body can't heal no more. That's okay; I've had my fun.

"There's no need to call the doctor, baby. Let's just get this dying done."

The set is finally over. Jimmy Ray disappears. Probably the men's room, Dagmar thinks, so she walks over to Jesus' table. "How's the iced tea?"

"He doesn't have much time left," Jesus says. "Hope you've made your peace with him." Two days and counting, he thinks.

"You're not much for small talk, are you?"

Jesus shrugs, "Just thought you should know."

They both watch as Jimmy Ray reappears from backstage to pack up his things. The old man is shaking a great deal. Sweating harder than he should.

This Jesus guy could be right, Dagmar thinks, and feels a spidery numbness crawl across her chest.

"I better go help," Jesus says.

When he leaves the table, Dagmar takes a plastic bag out of her pocket and uses it to pick up his empty glass. She shakes the ice into a plant. All she needs is the glass for fingerprints.

Not exactly Buddhist of her, she knows that, but a little caution is in Jimmy Ray's best interest. Dagmar woke up in the middle of the night suddenly worried. In all the confusion over Leon's death, she'd forgotten to mention Jesus to Trot. At 2 A.M. it occurred to her that the American Dream showed up the same day Jesus did. And Trot is worried about these Levi people who could be missing. So, even though the Jesus guy seems harmless, Dagmar knows it's better to check it out. Drop the glass by Trot's office.

It's the right thing to do, but Dagmar still feels guilty. Jimmy Ray really likes the man. Seems happier when he's around. She knows that as soon as she gives the glass to Trot, he'll play cop. Probably haul Jesus in for questioning on general principles. Then Jimmy Ray will give her the "bad Buddhist lecture" and be icy for at least a week.

Unless I don't tell Trot the real story about the prints, she thinks. I could say they belonged to some guy who drove away without paying. Make it seem like it's a favor. He'd buy that. Trot always believes me.

She looks back at the stage, and Jesus and Jimmy Ray are joking like old friends. They see her watching them and they both wave, arms around each other like Siamese twins. Then laugh. The guilt grinds her, but that's not uncommon. Everyone Dr. Ricardo Garcia encounters always feels a little guilty when they first suspect he's a murderer. It's only natural. He really isn't a bad guy, as far as serial killers go. He means well. People sense that. He wants to do what's right. And he's very helpful. Sure, he kills people. But he has manners, elegant manners. He knows his salad fork from the dessert. His parents made sure of it.

As a child, Dr. Ricardo Garcia was given all the best life had to offer. His father, Dr. Luis Garcia, was a wildly successful plastic surgeon in predominately white St. Petersburg, Florida. His mother, Maria Garcia, was a family practice doctor.

The Garcias were an attractive, popular family. They lived in a barrel-tiled Spanish house on a deep-water canal in the old money Snell Isle neighborhood. The country club district was well known for red brick streets that wrap genteelly around Coffeepot Bayou and flood in high rains—but flood with all the style that money can buy. They played tennis often. To the outside world, the Garcias were a successful prominent Cuban American family.

There was only one problem—they were actually Polish.

Luis and Maria, born Boguslaw and Jadwiga, were olive-skinned Poles who immigrated to this country right before Ricardo was born. They came to America for money. And sunshine. It was a fairly easy transition for them. They were successful doctors in Krakow and spoke many languages, including Spanish. They were also politically connected—and quite skilled at blackmail—so a diplomat who had a fondness for cross-dressing and small farmyard animals magically transferred their medical licenses. He extended them diplomatic immunity and made them the official physicians for the consulate in Miami. No further schooling or medical training was required.

The only snag came when a low-level immigration officer wondered "Why on this good green Earth" would someone from Poland want to change his or her name to "Garcia."

"It's like exchanging one problem for another. If you're going to change your name at all, most like "Smith." Something neutral like that," she offered. "Or "Brown." Or "Eisenhower." Everybody likes Ike."

The idea of taking the name of the then-current president did have a momentary appeal. However, in textbook Spanish, Luis said, "My wife wants to live in Florida. How many successful Polish doctors do you know in Florida?"

And so the Garcias came to be. They never stepped foot

in Miami, but moved to St. Petersburg because it had the fewest Cubans in the entire state. They wanted to refine their newly acquired ethnic heritage without question.

The scheme worked well until Ricardo turned ten years old, and Maria decided it was time to tell her son of their secret Polish heritage. Hoping to make her child understand the difficulty of their decision, she attempted to ease the shock with a meal that her mother used to make back in Poland.

With great love and devotion, Maria/Jadwiga explained each of the seven courses in both English and Polish. There was borscht made with cabbage and sausage; *Kielbasa,* a garlic sausage, served on a bed of sweet and sour red cabbage; cabbage rolls stuffed with sausage and mashed potatoes, and, of course, *perogis,* moon-shaped raviolis stuffed with mashed potatoes, cabbage, and sausage, then served with a white cream sauce. There were also herrings in cream sauce and sauerkraut with caraway seeds. And potato pancakes with chives. And lots of butter. And lots of sour cream. And three kinds of poppy seed cake for dessert.

It was July. The temperature was ninety-eight degrees with 98 percent humidity. It was also the 1960s—a time when air-conditioning was an inexact science.

"This was Sunday dinner in Krakow when I was a girl," his mother explained with a homesick lilt to her voice.

For a boy who grew up teething on mangos ("This is how we did it in Havana," his mother would tell her Snell Isle neighbors), the food of his real ethnic heritage had a profound impact on both his psyche and digestive system.

Ricardo spent the better part of two days doubled over in the bathroom.

The only comforting thought for the boy was that this revelation finally explained the unsettling first memory of his parents rocking him to sleep at night singing the "I Don't Want Her You Can Have Her She's Too Fat for Me" polka.

Still, the family secret gnawed at him. Eventually Ricardo found himself listening to Liberace and Bobby Vinton. He surreptitiously read everything he could about famous Poles like Fredric Chopin, Madame Curie, and the Polish American baseball great Stan Musial.

After a while, the pressure became too great. He began hearing voices. He began taking risks. He developed a fondness for mashed potatoes, poppy seed pastry, and plum preserves. On his twenty-first birthday, after being awarded a Harvard Medical School fellowship designed for Cuban refugees, he bought himself a button accordion.

And so, in the dead of night, urged on by voices only he could hear, he lurked in the alleyways of Harvard Square practicing such polka greats as the Flying Dutchmen's massive hit, "In Heaven There Is No Beer."

The double life had just become too much.

Chapter 25

There is something about the sight of Grover Cleveland in a tutu that would unhinge even the most sanguine man. But two hundred and fifty of them, prancing, hairy-chested in pink, were an embarrassment of psychotic riches. Plus, they were performing "Swan Lake." Over and over again. It wasn't a pretty delusion, but it was persistent. The only consolation for Leon was that Grover was a mighty fine dancer, even when multiplied to the two hundred fiftieth power. He hung in the air, seemingly magical. Effortless. Amazing.

Hospital drugs, Leon thought. Dang cool.

But Leon knew it was just about time to leave. After nearly a week in the hospital, and after being proclaimed Bee-Jesus by the news wire services ("Bewildered Bee-Jesus Be Found on Christmas Day"), and the apparition of the Virgin Mary—everything changed.

It rained. The Virgin Mary washed away.

Suddenly, the crowds of believers thinned. Nurse Becker decided to go back to the night shift. But that was all okay with Leon. He'd be happy if everybody left him alone. He liked lying in the clean white room drifting in and out of the puzzle of his life.

The only true believer who was left was Sam, who rolled in twice daily, often bringing gifts like old copies of *Sports Illustrated* that he'd stolen from the waiting room.

"Feel a miracle coming on?"

Leon had grown attached to the boy. Knew he would miss him when he went home—wherever the heck that was. The details of Leon's previous life were still a little fuzzy. A tiny voice in the back of his head kept saying, "Home is where the Clevelands are," but Leon couldn't imagine living in Cleveland. When he tried to imagine the city, all he could conjure up was a bitterly cold football stadium filled with people wearing stuffed brown dogs on their heads like hats—and barking.

He preferred two hundred and fifty Grover Clevelands dancing Swan Lake.

But he knew he'd have to figure it out soon. Little by little, the doctor was weaning him from the drugs. Soon, the tutued Clevelands would become a somewhat fond memory, and Leon would be out in the street. Or, worse yet, locked up in some state hospital like Chattahoochee—at least that's what Nurse Becker had told him.

"That's the Florida Asylum for the Insane," she explained sweetly. "But don't you worry, they haven't had nobody die from bilious dysentery in a very long time."

Facts like this made it difficult to concentrate. And all the interruptions—if it wasn't the dancing Clevelands with their hairy tree-stump legs effortlessly pirouetting, it was that *National Examiner* reporter Harlan Oakley.

Even though the Virgin Mary disappeared a few days ago, he seemed to be suddenly standing at the foot of Leon's bed, leaning over him, sniffing.

"You awake?"

For a first time in a long time Leon actually felt awake. "Sure," he said "But the show's over. The Virgin Mary washed away."

Oakley laughed. It was a cackle, actually. "And that's exactly why God invented Photoshop," he said. "A little digital retouching and I can have Castro himself walking on water."

Oakley was a tall lanky man with shock-blue eyes and rubber band arms. "Are you into snake handling? Because if you're Pentecostal that makes this story front-page material.

"Or levitating? If you could make something zip around the room that would be great. Bedpan would be impressive. A baby—even better."

Every question sounded like a negotiation to Leon. "Look," Leon said. "Just make something up. Isn't that what you people do?"

Oakley's blue eyes dimmed a few watts. "Those were the good old days," he said, wistful. "We used to have the corner on the fine art of interpretative journalism. "E.T. Holds Summit with Yetis"—that was my first. It was concise and yet, evocative."

A tear glistened in the man's eye.

"But now everybody's doing it: *New York Times, Boston Globe, Fox News.* They're muscling in. We're the ones who created imaginary sources. Where did they get off stealing that one from us?"

Leon shrugged.

"They ruined everything. Now, we have to *talk* to people—actually *interview* them—*speak* to them. Company rule. Ethics, they say. But what's all that talking going to get you? People are weird. It's scary talking to them. They don't always tell the truth. They make things up. I didn't become a journalist so that I could run around and talk to people. I'm just interested in the truth."

Oakley shuddered at the thought, and then sat down hard on the edge of Leon's bed. "In the old days," he said, "I could just sit at home and create the six-hundred-pound woman who gave birth to triplets after being pregnant for seven years. But these days, I have to find one. And they're usually not very nice people. And sometimes they're downright cranky. And rude. No manners at all. And I still have to *talk* to them.

"It's horrible. This used to be a gentleman's profession."

Leon was starting to feel sorry for Oakley until lunch arrived and the man snatched Leon's drumstick and began to eat it.

"So, here's the deal," Oakley said, chewing. "I don't mean to break your balls over this miracle thing, but New Year's Eve is tomorrow and we want to give the public a sense of hope for the New Year, don't we?" As he spoke, bits of chicken tumbled from his lips. "I mean, a great hopeful story means a bonus for me and a shot in the arm for everybody in general."

Oakley then picked up the corn muffin from Leon's tray. Swallowed it in two bites. Washed it down with the chocolate milk.

"I was going to drink that," Leon whined. He really wanted that chocolate milk.

Oakley looked at the tray. "There's still some Waldorf salad. Look there's apples, walnuts, coconut, and mayo. Looks good."

He picked up a spoon and offered some to Leon. "Come on," he said. "Open wide. Open your little hangar. I'm coming in for a landing."

Then he made a pretty convincing airplane sound, but Leon wasn't buying it.

"That's okay," Leon said. "I'm not hungry right now."

So Oakley ate it.

"So here's the deal," he said; a flake of coconut hung on his lip. "I'll be back about 3 P.M. with a camera. Maybe you can just lay hands on somebody and cure them. How about Gator Sam, that football kid? Tough break for that badass pecker, don't you think? We keep in touch. I was the one who dubbed him "Gator Sam.""

"Great story. 'The kid that nobody wanted' beats the crap out of a gator. Americana at its finest. But now look at him. Golden Boy turned golden loser—maybe you could just lay hands on him so I can write him into the story. I'll paint the Virgin back on the window and I'll write something like 'Even the miraculous Bee-Jesus couldn't cure Gator Sam—so he needs the public's help.'"

Oakley was on a roll.

"Cash will be pouring in for Gator Sam. What do you think? I think they'll eat it up in Des Moines."

While Mr. Oakley seemed to be perfectly capable of having both sides of this conversation on his own, he actually did notice that Leon looked less than enthusiastic.

"Okay. Look," Oakley said, "I'll be honest with you. I like the kid and the kid needs our help. This shithole of a hospital won't give him a leg for free. And the university told him to kiss off because he was drunk and never bought any of the student health insurance. They're cold, man. They took his brand-new Firebird, filled it full of his stuff, called a car transport service, and delivered it here to the hospital parking lot. How's that for icy? He was officially thrown out. Washed up. It's over. Kid was golden on the field, an angel in cleats—a royal SOB off. But nobody's perfect, so let's give the kid a break.

"So, you in?"

Leon cleared his throat, which Oakley took as yes. So he slapped Leon on the back. "Great. Great," Oakley said. "I'll be back in a couple of hours.

"By the way, get a sponge bath while I'm gone, okay? Nobody likes to see their savior looking like he's been drug through a swamp. Doesn't sell covers."

The door slammed behind him.

"But I *was* drug through the swamp." Leon whined.

That's when it came to him. I am Leon Pettit of Whale Harbor, Florida. I am the owner of the American Dream recreational vehicle worth about two hundred and fifty Clevelands, which do not dance and do not wear small sad dogs on their heads—but equate to two hundred and fifty thousand spendable American dollars.

It was, as they say, a breakthrough.

And then Sam rolled in.

"You got a pair of pants I could borrow?" Leon asked. "And how about your car, too?"

Chapter 26

As Mama Po had always predicted, Leon arrived late for his own funeral.

When he pulled into Whale Harbor it was just after 2 P.M. Leon was surprised to see cars at Lucky's RV Round-Up. Not just one car, but dozens. The lot was nearly filled. There was a sign out front that read "Funereal Bar-be-que. 2 P.M." It was in Bender's handwriting. The letters were perfectly square and appropriately somber. The air was thick with the fragrance of wood smoke and pig fat. Bob the Round-Up Cowboy was tossing his lasso out and coming up short, but laughing.

Leon was laughing, too. Happy to be so loved.

Happy that there was barbecue. Happy that his mandarin orange 1975 El Dorado was parked in front of Lucky's. Somehow, it was spared from the fire.

Thank God, Leon thought. Pimp Daddy Caddy is safe.

As was the Dream—it winked in the sunlight.

"You wait here," Leon told Sam and ran over to the RV as if it were a long-lost friend. There were tears in his eyes, and two hundred and fifty thousand Grover Clevelands dancing in his head, when he took the keys from behind the front tire where he left them. Everything seemed to be just as he had left it. The driver's door still opened with a whoosh.

"Shh, now," he said and took a quick check of the tiny freezer. The ice was still there. On the king-sized bed the little mouse pillows still smelled like lavender. The bedspread was rumpled, just the way he left it. So, with a quick hand, he smoothed it. It felt lumpy. He hadn't noticed that before.

"Like bricks or something," he thought and pulled up the mattress.

"Dang," he said. It was all he could think to say.

There was $350,000, still in bank wrappers and neatly arranged in a large space-age vinyl bag, taped to the bottom of the bed.

At any minute, Leon expected a hairy Grover Cleveland to appear in a tutu, arabesque-ing like a fat flamingo. But it was not a dream. Or residual hospital drugs. It was cash, and plenty of it.

"Dang."

At that moment, Leon felt a certain kinship with the bag. Felt as if the air had been sucked out of him, too. He looked out the window. The entire town appeared to be inside Lucky's. Leon waved at Sam. Sam frowned. Leon wanted to count the money, roll in it, but there was no time. Pretty soon the event would be over and everybody would be eating tiny barbecue sandwiches.

Leon kissed the bag. "Later," he whispered, amazed that all he had to do to get this lucky was die.

Had he known this earlier, he would have blown himself up years ago.

Leon then took off the XXXL T-shirt he borrowed from Sam and wrapped it around the money. Stuffed them both into the tiny washing machine. It'll be safe there, he thinks, nobody likes dirty laundry. Nobody will touch it.

Inside of Lucky's, there was plenty of beer. Kegs lined the showroom. Tables were filled with an assortment of salads, pies, and cakes. The showroom was crowded, every folding chair in town taken. People really wanted to get together and drink a few beers in Leon's honor. Tell a few lies. Barbecue a pig.

Trot had made the arrangements. "Best friends," everyone said. Which was true, but Trot also wanted to keep an eye on Jesus—or Dr. Ricardo Garcia as Trot now knew the man's name to be. Funerals are a good way to see who's hiding something. Trot still wasn't convinced that Leon's death was an accident. But until the medical examiner could run the DNA, that was more or less the official assumption.

"Next week," the ME promised.

Next week felt too late. Trot suspects that if Jesus showed up on Christmas Eve—as did the Dream—he may make a move tonight, on New Year's Eve. Sheet-fella has a flare for the dramatic, he thought, and wants to keeps a close eye on him. A "Funereal Bar-be-que," as Bender called it, seemed the perfect excuse.

Jimmy Ray and Jesus arrived together. They were both wearing coal black suits. Both looked like men who stopped by on their way to a better class of gathering—all Saks Fifth Avenue savvy and smiling. Trot wondered if Jimmy Ray knew that his new Jesus pal was a doctor. An insane doctor, but a medical man nonetheless. Trot made a note to pull Jimmy Ray aside and talk to him a little. Figure out what Doctor Jesus has been up to all these days.

So at 2 P.M. the Funereal Bar-be-que had begun. In the front row, Carlotta and Dagmar sat down together. The sight gave Trot pause.

How can they do that?

It wasn't easy. When Dagmar first saw Carlotta she didn't know how to feel or what to think. But Carlotta looked so alone sitting by herself in the back of the room with nobody to talk to. Dagmar couldn't have it.

"It's only right," she said and took Carlotta by the arm. "We'll sit together."

"Thanks," she whispered.

When the service began the two leaned into each other, shoulders touching, like sisters. Tried not to cry.

"My girl has a good heart," Jimmy Ray whispered to Jesus.

Jesus nodded. "A heart worthy of salvation."

Something about the way Jesus said that gave Jimmy Ray pause.

Trot planned a service, of sorts. He wanted to keep it simple, just something that spoke to the essence of Leon's life, but he wasn't quite sure what that would be, so he made sure there was plenty of beer. Bender offered to officiate.

"It will be my finest hour," he said and came wearing his best blue Hawaiian print shirt with a tie that featured a single hula girl captured middance, her hands over her eyes. He was the embodiment of Waikiki sorrow.

Bender had never given a eulogy before. He'd spent all night crafting it and was quite proud that he managed to tie together Dylan Thomas's "Do not go gentle into that good night," along with a snippet of Dante's *Inferno,* in Italian, and his own philosophy of life.

After he spoke, Jimmy Ray and the Blind Brothers' Blues Band planned to play the Eagles' "Tequila Sunrise," Leon's favorite song. They didn't know the song. Figured they'd just give it a go since most of the band, along with most of America, knew the chorus.

"We'll just go down and dirty it like Johnny Lee Hooker would do," Jimmy Ray said. "Lots of harmonica, lots of bass."

In honor of this musical interlude Bender's hair was now a sunrise of watermelon and mango Jell-O. Looked radioactive.

Since there wasn't a body to view, Trot took Leon's melted wraparound sunglasses and placed them on a folding chair with a sign that read "Leon," just in case somebody thought it was trash.

Dagmar placed a handful of magnolia blossoms next to the chair. Carlotta, a passion fruit flower crown.

So now, about a half an hour into the event, the Funereal Bar-be-que is, as Jimmy Ray leans over and whispers to Jesus, "roasting and toasting."

Bender, with his tequila sunrise hair, had already recited Dylan Thomas, spoken Italian, and was now barking like a loopy golden retriever.

"You may ask why I bark at a time such as this," he says to the fifty or so assembled. "I have recently come to barking because I believe it is a form of prayer. I bark to honor my inner dog."

Then he barks again. This time it's a dark poodle of a rumble.

"You see, we are loved and nourished by mysterious hands, the hands of our master—be it God, Buddha, Shiva—whatever the name—they got your kibbles. They got your bits."

The crowd nods.

"Can somebody give me a bark?" Bender asks.

Carlotta lets out a tentative yip.

"That's good," Bender says. "Cocker spaniel?"

She smiles.

"Anybody a bull mastiff?"

A couple of huge barks come from the back of the room.

"King Charles? Beagles? Collies?"

There are assorted barks and yips, which only serves to encourage the mayor.

"Sometimes," he says, "you have to try on one or two barks before you get it right."

Then he points at Mrs. Sitwell, who is neither barking nor smiling. "Corgi!" he says to her. "Welsh corgi! Give it a go, Mrs. Sitwell. Unleash your inner corgi!"

Everyone is watching her. Waiting. So she yaps a snippy little yap like a Pembroke on a bad day.

Bender is ecstatic. "Wonderful! Everybody bark now! Let us all bark in memory of that old red coonhound Leon who is now sitting at the right hand of his god, whatever or whoever he or she or it may be, getting a gigantic scratch behind the ears."

And one by one everyone at the Funereal Bar-be-que joins in. Some are pointers. A couple are pugs.

It sounds a lot like feeding time at the Humane Society.

Everybody is so busy barking that nobody notices Leon, who is bruised, shirtless, and wearing pants at least four sizes too large, slip in the side door of the showroom with the lumbering Gator Sam. Sam is wobbly on his crutches, whispers to Leon, "These people are crazy."

Leon smiles. "Sweet, ain't it?"

He's locked up the American Dream and can feel the key pressed against his leg. He can't stop thinking about it—*Got to be thousands of shrink-wrapped dollars. Jesus loves me. Really loves me.* So he barks that high-pitched frantic "Treed-Me-A-Fat-Opossum-And-Life-Is-Good" bark that only a red coonhound can bark.

And it feels good, so good that when everyone else is finished, Leon is still barking.

I'm rich. I'm stinking rich.

His inner dog is clearly out of control.

Dagmar is the first to recognize the sound of Leon's voice, dog that he is.

When she turns and sees him—his naked chest, Sam's huge blue jeans tied around his waist, his chin up and yapping—she throws her head back and laughs, mostly out of relief.

"That crazy son of a bitch," she says.

"Leon!" Carlotta shouts and runs to him.

"Shoot," Jimmy Ray says.

Trot, out of reflex, takes out his gun and aims.

Everyone turns and Leon stops barking, but Sam, always a little slower than most, begins. He's decided on an Old English sheepdog. A dense, definitive bark.

In all the confusion, Jesus slips away.

Chapter 27

Over the past two years, Dr. Ricardo Garcia left a trail of bodies that would impress even the most experienced law enforcement officers—if only they knew. But nobody ever suspected the doctor. Many of his victims were patients who were near death anyway, seemed to die in their sleep. The rest were people that nobody missed. Angelo, the male nurse, "The First," had continually threatened to quit if he didn't get a raise. So, when he didn't show up for work, the hospice assumed he'd made good on his threat. And none of his ex-wives seemed to miss him at all.

"Ten" was a problem, though. "Ten" was the lawyer in charge of Dr. Garcia's family estate. "Ten" was William David, attorney-at-law and probate specialist.

The vole-faced man, who never made eye contact, had just helped Dr. Ricardo Garcia's frail mother sign herself into a nursing home. As a ward of the state, her considerable fortune was under Mr. David's control. When Dr. Garcia arrived at the home, he was told that his mother did not wish to see him. He called her repeatedly, but she wouldn't take the calls. So he called the lawyer.

"Why wasn't I notified?"

"Legally, this is none of your business. She committed herself. She was sane. It is her right as an adult," he said. Then hung up.

So Dr. Garcia had no choice.

In retrospect, this was his finest hour. Messy but brilliant. The lawyer's office was in a rickety old Victorian house with a wraparound porch that overlooked Tampa Bay. No security cameras or guards. Lots of windows. The probate specialist was a habitual man, worked late, and could often be seen going into the kitchen to pour himself a cup of coffee around midnight.

The plan was simple. The window over the kitchen sink was often left open a crack. All the doctor had to do was lift himself in, put a few drops of fentanyl in the coffeepot, and William David, attorney-at-law and probate specialist, would die. Neatly. Quietly. Quickly.

Unfortunately, it would not be painful.

This fact vexed Dr. Garcia, but he had no choice. Even

the voices inside his head had to agree that fentanyl was the perfect "Tool of Salvation" for the occasion. It's a powerful drug, a synthetic opiate, one hundred times stronger than morphine. It's mostly used on terminal patients, like those at the hospice, so he had easy access to it. And since it's so dangerous it's rarely prescribed. Medical examiners don't usually test for it.

So it was a perfect plan. Tainting the coffee was easier than imagined. Someone had left the kitchen door unlocked. Dr. Garcia slipped in without even a creak from the floorboards. Drugged the pot. Hid in the broom closet. Waited.

At midnight, William David, attorney-at-law and probate specialist, poured his coffee and took it back to his office. Blew on it. Took a sip. Looked surprised. Slumped.

It was perfect, but anticlimatic.

Luckily, the probate specialist was a pen collector. Fountain pens worth thousands of dollars sat in a display case on the desk. Dr. Garcia was inspired.

With a ruby-encrusted fourteen-karat gold Montblanc in his skilled latex-gloved hand, he carefully crafted a tattoo, a quote from Shakespeare—"First Kill the Lawyers"— across the probate specialist's scrawny volelike chest.

The mess was incredible. Blood was everywhere. But an artist never minds inconvenience, he told himself.

Unfortunately, halfway though the process, William David, attorney-at-law and probate specialist, surfaced from the drug-induced coma.

He was not a man who appreciated whimsy.

And so he, as Dr. Garcia would later come to think of it, put up quite a fuss.

Still, in the end, the doctor managed to pour the rest of the fentanyl-laced coffee down the man's throat. Finish the tattoo. Clean up. Leave.

The doctor is a very neat man. Does impeccable work. Only a single hair was left behind. Now, six months later, with at least 322 possible suspects, no one has even interviewed Dr. Garcia yet. There isn't an APB out for him. In fact, he's clean—which makes Dagmar even more surly.

"How is that possible? How can he *not* have a record?"

She's been sitting in Trot's cramped office prodding him ever since she followed him back after Leon's funeral. She wants some answers. Won't give up.

Trot shrugs. "I don't know."

"You don't know, or aren't telling me?"

"The effect is the same," he says.

Trot's desk is tiny, but immaculate. All the appropriate forms are in the "in" or "out" or "pending" box. Dagmar's eyes narrow. She puts her hand on Trot's "pending box" and holds it there like a discus thrower. This is not good, Trot thinks. It's clear that she wants to toss his perfect paperwork out the window.

"We have to do something," she says.

He gently moves her hand away. "We?" he asks. "Since when is this a 'we' situation?"

"Since you told me about the Levis. Since Leon won the Dream. Since I let this Jesus guy into my car."

Dagmar has not been in a good mood since Jesus disappeared.

"Look," Trot says, "it's not clear that Dr. Garcia has done anything except have a nervous breakdown and somehow manage to take possession of a fancy RV. He could have bought it. It could be that simple."

They both know this is not the truth. The lie feels uneasy between them.

"You're still sore about those fingerprints, aren't you?" Dagmar says. "I didn't mean to trick you, telling you some guy stiffed The Café."

"You didn't," Trot says. "I didn't believe you."

Her face colors.

"Look, I'm not being stubborn, as you put it," he continues on. "I'm just being sheriff because I am. It's my job."

"But we can place Rose Levi at the scene."

"There's no 'we.' There's no scene. I'm not even sure there's been a crime."

Dagmar knows he's lying and he is. Trot is absolutely sure that Dr. Garcia murdered the old couple. As soon as Trot identified the fingerprints, he called Tampa. According to a police report, Rose Levi, in her haste to take full advantage of the Early Bird Specials at the famed Columbia Restaurant in Ybor City, backed the American Dream over Dr. Garcia's white picket fence and effectively squashed his mailbox. The report then stated that Mrs. Levi of Cicero wanted to file a complaint against Dr. Garcia for having a mailbox that distracted drivers.

"It jumped out at me," she was quoted as saying.

Apparently, a gust of wind caught the "General Practice" sign, and Mrs. Levi mistook it for a low flying egret and swerved. She narrowly missed the tricked-out yellow

Olds sedan airbrushed with the faces of rap stars, but nailed the said mailbox. Not a scratch on the Dream.

The report also stated that Mrs. Levi cursed a good deal and referred to Dr. Garcia by several "colorful" ethnic terms.

It was also noted that Mr. Levi was mostly silent throughout the investigation. He did, however, ask Mrs. Levi repeatedly if it was, "Time for my highball yet, sweetie?"

"I would have killed her," the cop from Tampa said. "Him, too. Get your own damn highball, you old coot."

"But would Garcia?" Trot asked.

"According to the report, this Dr. Garcia was pretty well mannered. A real charmer. So the squad left."

And the Levis stayed. And a month later the Levis are missing and Garcia believes he's Jesus and he's driving their RV.

Of course, the doctor killed them. All Trot needs is proof. But he's not going to tell Dagmar any of this. He knows she's read one too many Nancy Drew books, a couple of which he now regrets giving her for her fourteenth birthday. *Password to Larkspur Lane* and *The Clue in the Diary* were her favorites, and Trot's, too. He always thought the Hardy Boys played a little too rough.

"Look," he says. "This is an official investigation. You have to get out of my office and let me handle it. Let this go."

"But how would this doctor get the RV without killing them?"

"Leon says Garcia is some sort of a poker genius. He could have invited Irv and Rose in. Then fleeced them."

"But if he didn't kill them, where are they? Wouldn't they have gotten to Miami by now?"

"I don't know."

"If he was so good at poker, how does he lose to Leon?"

"I don't know."

"Well, maybe he let Leon win because he's trying to get rid of evidence."

"Could be. Can't get a warrant without a complaint though."

"Won't Leon just let you take a look?"

"Says the keys were burned up in the fire."

"And you don't believe him?"

"Do you?"

They both know the answer, and it is not improving Dagmar's mood. Buddha heart, my ass—she keeps thinking to herself—the guy's a killer and I invited him for Christmas.

Trot is trying not to lose his temper but it's getting difficult. The trail is getting cold. He has to get rid of Dagmar. It's too dangerous for her if she tags along. And he doesn't want her following him. "Look," he says. "This Jesus guy is long gone. What matters is that Jimmy Ray is safe. You're safe. Don't you have to work tonight? It's New Year's Eve. Big night, right?"

"It's my fault he's even here."

About now, it's clear to Trot that he's going to have to arrest her to get her out of his office. He's pretty sure she won't like that. Pretty sure he should come up with a better solution. "Can I ask something?" he says. "Something I've been wondering about?"

Dagmar looks a little apprehensive. "Sure," she says, but doesn't sound sure.

He leans back in his chair, appears to settle in. "Ever since Leon's service, I've been thinking about my inner dog. What do you think? Golden retriever? Great Dane? St. Bernard—wait, too much hair. How about one of those big Newfoundland dogs? They save people all the time. What do you think? What kind of dog am I?"

Dagmar is squirming. The one thing she hates most in the world is small talk. Trot knows that. That's what he's counting on.

"I mean of all the dogs," he continues. "What kind of dog am I?"

Dagmar looks at him as if he's suddenly deranged.

Housebroken, she thinks.

"I better go," she says and closes the door firmly behind her.

"Well, Miss Dagmar," Trot says to the door, "I've got you figured for a chow." Then he barks a regal, loyal, and somewhat menacing bark in her honor.

Chapter 28

On the morning Sam the Gator came to Whale Harbor, he'd finally reached his sports agent. The conversation did not go well. In fact, it didn't go at all.

"Kid—the fat lady. She sang," the agent said and hung up.

That's why Sam came. "It's not over until it's over," he wanted to tell the agent, but Sam was actually pretty sure it was over. So he needed a miracle more than anything. Or at least, something that seemed like a miracle to the readers of the *National Examiner*. That's why he rolled back into the Bee-Jesus' room, loaned him a pair of his own pants, and then let him drive his brand-new Firebird to a town that he'd never heard of—a town where people bark at funerals, a town where there's supposed to be a real Jesus.

But there isn't one. The Jesus in question has disappeared. And Leon, with Sam's blue jeans tied up around his waist, looks a lot like Jethro Bodine on the lam from Miss Hathaway. Not like a mystical Bee-Jesus at all.

When Mr. Oakley arrives, Sam thinks, he is going to be real pissed at me.

Things were not exactly looking up for the former football star. So Sam lay down on the sagging plaid couch in Leon's office and tried to think of his next move.

Despite Leon's untimely rise from the dead, the memorial service continued on in the showroom. "No sense to ruin a party," Bender proclaimed. So the Blind Brothers' Blues Band played "Mustang Sally." Bender did the moonwalk with Mrs. Sitwell. Carlotta ignored the men and did a slow and sultry version of the watusi by herself. Dagmar stood in the corner with her cell phone and made calls. The keg of beer was untapped. Leon was deep in conversation with Trot.

Sam didn't know what to do. Didn't know anybody. Couldn't dance. So he hobbled into Leon's office and lay on the couch; the springs creaked under his weight. He'd taken his last meds before lunch, four hours ago. What was left of his leg was now throbbing. The wound, which he picked at, was bleeding though the bandage. The couch smelled like an incontinent cat.

Sam closed his eyes and tried not to think about it, but the music in the next room, and the laughter, made him angry. He knows he should be dancing and drinking but not with losers like these, but with models and cheerleaders. And not in a loser town like Whale Harbor, but in New York City, or Detroit, or Dallas. He knows he should be in a town that can appreciate somebody who, even with a fake leg, is better than William the Refrigerator Perry ever was. Sam the Gator is better, and he knows it. He is faster and stronger. He is the best that ever played the game. And he knows it is just a matter of time before the Jets, or Bucs, or Patriots will understand that—agent or no agent.

"Shit, I don't need anybody," he says, but there isn't anybody around to hear him.

As the Blind Brothers' Blues Band kicks into a wily winking version of "She's a Brick House," Sam tries to recall the last touchdown he made, just a month ago, at the bowl game. Usually when he does this, he can close his eyes and feel the crowd cheering in his bones. But not now. Now, he just feels big and dull. Slowed. The pain in his leg is too much. Keeps his eyes closed, anyway. Tries not to focus on the pain.

"Hey Gator man," Leon whispers, gently shakes him. "Wake up."

Sam opens his eyes. "Not asleep."

Leon is standing over him. He is still bare-chested and now grinning like a jack-o'-lantern. He's holding two plastic cups—sweet tea for Sam, and a beer for himself.

"Apparently people love me," Leon says and hands Sam the iced tea. "It's good to be dead."

The pain in Sam's leg makes him dizzy, confused. "Hey, what happened to my T-shirt?" He just noticed that Leon was nearly naked.

"It's in the washing machine. I like things clean."

Sam frowns. "You are one ugly old man without a shirt, dude." Then he drinks the iced tea in one large gulp. Crushes the empty cup and hands it back to Leon. Then takes his beer from him.

"You don't happen to have any morphine, do you?" Sam says.

"No. Give me that beer. You're not twenty-one."

Sam gives him an ugly look. Coughs. Spits on the floor. "I'm in pain, man. Don't screw with me."

"All right. Hang on," Leon says and takes a bottle of generic aspirin from his top drawer. Tosses it to Sam, who catches it with one hand.

"Shit," Sam says. "The Vikings would weep if they saw that. I'm in a freakin' world of pain, and I still can catch with one hand." He shakes out a handful of pills.

"I think the recommended dosage is two," Leon says. "They're extra strength."

"Thanks," Sam says. "So am I."

Sam washes down the handful of aspirin with the dregs of Leon's beer.

Leon doesn't like the look of this. "Let me take you back to the hospital," he says and thinks of Nurse Becker who is probably worried—and maybe in trouble, too. He'd hate to see that.

Nice gal, he thinks. Hope she doesn't get fired.

"No way. I'm waiting for Oakley. I called him. He's going to help us find that Jesus fellow—even though he's still a little pissed that we ran out on him."

Damn, Leon thinks. That's all I need. I've got a shrink-wrapped bag of cash, and now that Oakley reporter is on his way. Leon sits down on the edge of his desk. Why did I let this kid talk me into taking him?

"You know," Leon says, "you should just call Oakley back. Turns out this Jesus guy's real name is Ricky Garcia, or something like that. He's like a doctor. Or was. There's no story."

"That doesn't mean anything. He can still be a Miracle Guy."

Leon thinks about Dr. Garcia's Bible eyes, the money-lender-at-the-temple glare.

"I don't think so. I think he's just a whack job."

The enormous boy is not deterred. "Is that what that loser sheriff was telling you? That loser sheriff guy with the lame comb-over? I saw you two talking."

Leon looks back at Trot, who has stopped to talk to Carlotta on his way out. Trot runs a hand through his sadly thinning hair as if trying to arrange it, but he's just generating static electricity. Wispy, it stands on end. Makes him look like he's been electrocuted. But Carlotta doesn't seem to notice. She looks happy, happier than Leon's ever seen her look.

"I don't know. Jeeter's a pretty smart guy," Leon says.

Just then Trot touches Carlotta's shoulder. She laughs. Dagmar puts her arm around him, pushes him out the door.

Both of them, Leon thinks. Trot's got both of them now. Great.

"Yep. That Sheriff Jeeter's a pretty smart guy," he says. "*Bastard* that he is."

"Guy's a loser. So are you," Sam says. "Go on with your loser life. Me, I'm waiting for the real Miracle Guy. This Jesus guy."

Leon turns back to see the massive boy is looking at him just the way Miss Pearl did the night before the men took her away. Makes him flinch.

"I got to go for a little while," he says. Carlotta told him about Grammy Lettie's house, the ghost house. "You stay right here—"

"Don't you want to know why you're a loser?" The boy is sneering at him.

"I've got a pretty clear bead on that, son."

Still, Sam is going to tell him anyway. "You really think I believe in this Jesus guy, don't you? Well, I don't. I never even believed that you were some Miracle Guy, either. I had you fooled the whole time. Just like I got that Oakley guy from the newspaper fooled. He's going to write it all up about me—"The Next Refrigerator Perry Asks Jesus for a Leg Up"—it's a great headline—even if the guy isn't Jesus. It's the kind of headline that can have me starting with the Packers—midwesterners love crap like that."

Sam is red-faced and desperate. The moment feels too raw. The two men just look at each other. Leon shakes his head a little. Can you say "howdy"? he thinks.

"Look, I've got an errand to run," he says. "I'll be back in a few."

Sam is afraid of being left alone again. A moment of panic crosses his face, and then he's back in charge. Or so he thinks.

"Just bring me a couple of beers," he orders. "And have one of the good-looking women check up on me every ten minutes or so. We need to keep that beer coming."

Leon leaves Sam with a fresh cup of sweet tea, which the boy unfortunately uses to take yet another handful of aspirin. The beers never come. The women never come. After a while, the aspirins take hold and Sam feels dizzy, nauseated. He's overdosed and his heart is racing, ears ringing. He's had too many aspirins, nearly half the bottle, but now, in his confusion, he takes a few more.

Suddenly, Sam has an overwhelming desire to lie on the beach in the late afternoon sun. He pulls himself onto his crutches and hobbles out the back door. Nobody notices. Even though the salt air is cool and dry, he's sweating profusely, lurching. The crutches slip as he walks. The bandage on his leg is spotty and unraveling. The shore is much farther than he expects it to be, even though it's really not that far at all. It's just a few feet behind Lucky's through a field of sea oats and sandspurs. Sam's in so much pain, and so confused, that he can hardly make it. He can barely hobble. A few feet from the shore, he trips. Hits the sand hard. Breaks his nose.

He lies there bleeding for a few moments. He is in trouble. He knows it, but won't give in, won't cry out for help.

It takes every bit of effort for the large boy to roll over. The waves crash over him, cold. Make him shake. A large wave crashes over him, pulls his crutches away. Slowed by pills, he cannot reach for them fast enough. They roll in and out with the tide.

He is beached on the shore. Gigantic. Pale. Belly-up.

Sam closes his eyes. Sleep comes clammy and rigid. He dreams only of rain. When a hand brushes the hair away from his face, he's not sure if he's still asleep.

"Have you ever been baptized?" a dark voice says.

Jesus, Sam thinks and opens his eyes.

Except for the fact that the man is holding a machete and wearing an expensive Egyptian cotton shirt tied around his bony waist like a loincloth, he does look like Jesus. At least, the Jesus Sam remembers his foster mother showing him in a picture book.

"Do I have to be baptized to get me a miracle?" Sam asks.

"It's the only way. But don't worry. It will end all earthly pain."

And Jesus is right. It does.

Chapter 29

"**Y**ou pays your money, you takes your chances."

Leon had forgotten about that old sign. It's written in Grammy Lettie's perfect Palmer Method handwriting, which she was always quite proud of. The sign gives him a sentimental feeling. For a moment, he wants to take it down and hang it over the front door at Lucky's, but then thinks better of it. Fair warning has a tendency to be bad for business.

"You need some time alone there," Carlotta told him. "Place feels haunted, but in a good way. Like your mama and grandma just want to remind you where you came from." Then she kissed

Leon on the cheek. That's when he knew it was probably over. He wanted to tell her about the shrink-wrapped money he found, but didn't. Leon could see by the way Carlotta stole a look at Trot that the money wouldn't make much difference anymore. It wasn't like he didn't see it coming, though.

Damn this town, he thinks. If only she hadn't expected whales.

So when everybody was dancing, Leon took the huge bag of money from the Dream's washing machine and stuffed it into his trunk. Didn't tell a soul.

On the way out to his family's former alligator farm, he made a list of all the things he needed to do now that he's not dead—and probably single again.

First—get some clothes. Running around shirtless without shoes and wearing jeans that are so big they make you look like a refugee from Ringling Brothers is not the best look for a man who recently came into a sack of shrink-wrapped cash.

Second—drag some gators back into Grammy Lettie's front yard and flood it up a little bit; not so much like the last time, just enough so the gators don't die.

Third—build an amphitheater around the whole thing.

Fourth—rename the place "The Ghost House Gator Farm."

Dang, I'm good, he thought. Who wouldn't pay money to see large amphibious creatures in the front yard of a house that's been spit back up from the earth?

Best of all, lucky thrill-seekers could have an opportunity to spend an hour training with one of the most famous gator wrestlers in the state of Florida—"Sam the Gator," former U of F football star. After a quick lesson, they could wrassle their own gator for only $250 a pop.

Cash in advance. No checks or credit cards, please.

Leon knew he was getting a little ahead of himself—he hadn't even talked to Sam about the idea—but he could smell the money rolling in. Extreme sports—everybody loves them. Swimming with sharks. Driving through Miami during tourist season. Even on TV, people are always lowering themselves upside down into snake pits and eating maggots. It's a fine American tradition.

This idea is foolproof, Leon thought. Which he knew meant that, even with a bag full of shrink-wrapped cash, he had about a 50-50 chance of pulling it off.

But now he's not so sure anymore. Not sure if he wants to.

As he walked through the arch of passion fruit flowers that wove themselves across the canopy of live oaks, he suddenly felt like he did when the bees had covered him. The air was fragrant, cool. His body hummed.

The house was smaller than he had imagined. Worn.

But still. There it was.

It's haunted in a good way, Carlotta told him.

The ghost house has risen, Trot had said.

Standing in the shadow of the gigantic gator grin—an entrance gate like no other, as Grammy Lettie used to say—Leon understands what they meant. He imagines the ghosts of Mama Po and Grammy Lettie sitting at the kitchen table playing five-card stud, no limit, just waiting to deal him in. So he goes inside.

The old-styled television makes him laugh. And there's TV tables just like the ones he has—or had.

"Had," he says out loud, and tries to get used to the word. Let it sink in. After the explosion, he officially has no place to live. Takes some getting used to.

Maybe I should just move in here, he thinks. Carlotta probably is going to move on soon. It's better than sleeping at Lucky's. Or in the Dream—those Levis could have been killed in there.

He hadn't thought of that before. The idea makes his skin go cold. He wraps his arms around his bare chest and thinks of the RV salesman's motto, "Ignorance is bliss," but isn't too sure about that anymore. In fact, he doesn't feel sure about much anymore. Everything feels changed. Even him.

And the house feels so quiet it spooks him. He didn't expect that. No hum from lights or electricity. Feels a little like church. Leon runs a hand though his tarnished hair and wishes he'd borrowed a shirt from Trot or Bender. Being bare-chested in such a quiet place seems disrespectful.

In the kitchen, however, there are no ghosts—at least none that he can see. The room smells of bleach and that smell he remembers as a kid, that particular mix of dying fish, heat, and salt. He likes that. Makes him happy.

The kitchen is good-sized, big and square, with an enameled stove. It's the kind of kitchen you can make tapioca in. Carlotta's left some plates in the sink. There's a coffee cup with her lipstick on it. The plates are milky green glass, as is the cup. Leon opens the cupboard, and there's a whole set of them. Not just plates and coffee cups, but juice glasses made from blue glass. A couple of jelly jars. Everything smells of bleach.

Carlotta at work, he thinks, and picks up a soup bowl. Holds it to his ear like a shell. Listens.

He's not sure what he's listening for, or why. But knows his mama must have had soup from this bowl—and Grammy Lettie, too. So he listens, but all he can hear is the sound of his own heart beating just a little too fast.

Haunted, he thinks, but in a good way.

Next to the living room is a small bedroom. He suspects it was Mama Po's; the walls are peeling pink paint. In the closet there are hangers with dresses, but the cloth of them is nearly rotted away; only shreds of fabric remain, colorless, bleached by salt air and water. The rotted fabric sways in the still air.

He opens the top drawer of her dresser. It creaks. The clothes inside are moldy and decayed, but on the top of them there's a bundle of something. A faded red ribbon is tied around what looks to be a stack of envelopes. Maybe love letters. It's tough to tell. The pages are so covered with mold and warped; the bundle is curled into itself. Looks like a small bird, long dead.

Leon's afraid to touch it. He tells himself whatever secrets are in this house they don't matter anymore. Still, when he looks around the peeling room, his chest goes tight.

Outside, he hears a bark, then a yip. From the window, he can see a family of panthers running along the beach, a mother and three kittens. Carlotta told him they were around. The cats are biting each other's ears and rolling in the surf as they make their way down the thin shoreline. They look happy. Leon watches from the window until he can't see them anymore. Then he goes outside after them, not willing to let them disappear quite yet.

They remind him of Cal, that roughneck, fearless way he used to play.

Just a minute more, he thinks. But by the time Leon reaches the water, the cats are scampering into a thick of cypress trees farther down the shoreline. Leon stands in the surf and watches them until they are out of sight. The tide is high and rough. There's a storm in the Gulf. Clouds bump up against each other and bruise. Waves break against Leon. He rocks under their force.

The peninsula of land that Lettie's house sits on curves like a hook. In the distance, Leon can see the neon light of Bob the Round-Up Cowboy. Can see the entire beach of Whale Harbor. The town looks so tiny and faraway. Hardly seems real.

The storm picks up. Lightning spins across the sky like so many spiderwebs. Leon can smell the coming rain. It's hard to leave, though. He tries to imagine what it was like when Mama Po was a girl and the town of Whale Harbor was really a town. Must have been able to see the lights of the Ferris wheel from here, he thinks.

The enormous blue jeans he borrowed from Sam are

taking in water quickly. The belt he's tied around his waist slips. A wave slaps him hard and the weight of the water pulls the pants around his knees.

Now he's naked.

This is not good.

This is the third time in a week that Leon has found himself alone and naked. The first time his trailer blew up. The second, a swarm of bees mistook him for a log. Now what? Obviously, being naked is a sign of bad luck.

Men aren't supposed to be naked when they're by themselves, he thinks. It's unnatural. Dangerous. *Hinky.*

He tries to pull Sam's pants up, but they're too heavy and are now filling with sand.

"If this is the way my life is going to go, I've got to get a hobby, man," he mumbles, but the only hobby he can think of is model railroading—all those tiny trains going round and round in circles—going nowhere fast. Sam's clown-sized pants palpitate around his ankles like a jelly-fish and Leon can imagine himself living alone, landscaping cardboard mountains, and wearing a conductor's cap.

He impersonates a train whistle, just for practice. "Woo-woo." A school of pinfish quickly scoots by him. And now he's really worried. He thinks he may like that sound.

He tries to pick up Sam's pants again, and a bolt of lightning cracks toward town. He looks up and sees something in the distance. Something large is in the water. It's too far to see what it is. But it looks white.

Whale.

"I'll be damned."

The white body arches in the high waves, then hits the water hard. Not graceful, as you'd expect. Seems to be struggling, but it's difficult for Leon to tell. The storm clouds have turned the sky muddy. If he squints, all he can see is something pale and large, thrashing.

"Got to be whales, though," Leon says, excited as a kid. "What else could it be?"

With all his strength, he pulls Sam's sinking pants up around his waist. Clenches his fist tightly to hold them in place. He's got to borrow some pants that fit better. Then find Carlotta.

"Every woman deserves whales," he says.

As Leon runs, he trips on the pant legs. Falls hard. Doesn't matter, though. There are whales in Whale Harbor. Life is good after all.

Chapter 30

For Jesus, "Thirteen" turned out to be a very lucky number indeed. Very quick. Very easy. Surprisingly so.

Unfortunately, there was a witness.

"Step away," Trot shouts, gun drawn.

Jesus is holding the machete in one hand. In the other is Sam. The boy's blue eyes are open and unseeing. "I saved him," Jesus says with that poker voice of his.

"Drop the knife in the water," Trot shouts. He tries not to focus on the dead boy; it's too late for him. Trot tries not to panic.

I'm sorry, he thinks over and over again. Hopes Sam can hear him in heaven.

"I gave him a proper baptism, like John the Baptist would," Jesus shouts. "I have given him the gift of salvation."

The boy's enormous pale body bobs up against Jesus as he speaks. The water around him is red from blood. The boy's face is nearly shredded, but Trot stares at Jesus. Doesn't break eye contact. Trot never had to shoot a man before, isn't afraid of it, but he doesn't want to make a mistake. Wants to give him every chance. The guy needs help. He's sick. Do it by the book, Trot tells himself.

"Drop the knife," he says again.

Jesus moves closer. "You believe in salvation?"

"Drop it."

Trot's hand is steady. He's aiming at Jesus' heart, but the tide is coming in. The waves are pounding the shore— Trot and Jesus, too. Both men move back and forth in the rough water. They look like drunks, stagger with each wave. Even this close, it would be difficult for Trot to get off a clear shot in such strong surf.

Jesus moves even closer. Trot can smell that sticky sweet blood smell.

"Don't," Trot shouts. "Just drop the knife. Let the body go."

Jesus smiles and releases Sam's body. Waves break over it. Pull it toward shore.

"Now the knife," Trot says. Steady.

A large wave hits Jesus from behind and covers him for a moment. He spits saltwater, staggers forward. Now he's within striking distance, just a blade away. "Everybody wants to be saved, isn't that right?" he says. "Even you."

"I'll give you to ten."

Trot is beyond fear, working on adrenaline. He keeps thinking about Sam, his huge body being washed on shore like some fish, but doesn't break eye contact.

"Nine. Eight. Seven."

"Fine," Jesus says and holds his arms out to Trot as if to surrender, but the machete still in his right hand. The waves push and pull harder. He stares at Trot with those Bible eyes. Unblinking.

"The knife," Trot says. "Just drop it."

"Of course."

And then, finger by finger, Jesus opens his hand. He is clear-eyed and smiling. The waves beat against his back.

Trot, sensing it's over, lowers his gun slightly.

But it's not over.

Chapter 31

In all of his forty-one years on this earth, Leon has never borrowed pants from another man before—now he feels as if he's making it a habit.

"Woo-woo," he says to himself. He's starting to really like the sound of a model train whistle. "Woo-woo."

And even Leon knows this is not a good sign.

Leon is standing in Bender's tiny living room, waiting for the mayor to find him pants that fit. He's clutching Sam's around his waist, feels naked. Hinky. Saltwater trickles down his leg, gives him goose bumps. He has sand in places that he's never had sand in before.

Bender lives in a small shed of a house behind The Pink. Inside, it looks like the singsong chalkboard in Mrs. Sitwell's former fifth-grade classroom; every available space is filled with aquariums. In his spare time, Bender breeds "designer" koi for the Japanese market. Five thousand dollars for one fish alone. Some of his most popular "mutations," as he calls them, are in his "Fishy Politicians" line. It's a bipartisan success. Bill Clinton and George W. Bush are both top sellers. The fish bear an uncanny resemblance to the men.

"It's all in the cheeks," Bender says. He's heard that they're sometimes used for sushi, but, being a politician himself, he tries not to think about that too much.

All those fish give the room a slightly green tint, an algae air. It's sort of like how Leon feels—green and musty.

"A complete ensemble," Bender says when he finally emerges from behind the beaded curtain of his bedroom. He hands Leon a towel to dry off with along with a pair of yellow golfing pants and a Hawaiian print shirt from his seemingly endless collection of Hawaiian print shirts.

"You *do* know we don't live in Hawaii?" Leon asks.

"I prefer to overlook insignificant details," Bender says and leaves the room so that Leon can dress. Both the shirt and pants are the color of police Caution tape. The shirt has splotches of red hibiscus on it.

Once dressed, Leon looks like a crime scene.

Bender sticks his head through the beaded curtain, "Fetching!" he says. Beaming.

Bender's also changed his clothes. He's now wearing a

black kimono with a frowning, squatting tiki god across the back of it, traditional *Zori* sandals, and white socks. He's sprayed his tequila sunrise hair with silver glitter. He is neon elegant. His wardrobe is inspired by a bartender he once knew in *Kabukicho,* Tokyo's red-light district, during the height of his "Pirate Years" with Jacques Cousteau.

"Hate to push you out," Bender says. "But it's New Year's Eve at The Pink. Lots to do. Stop by later. I'll pour you one on the house."

"What about the whales?" Leon asks. "In the harbor."

"Has to be something else. Harbor's too shallow. It'd be a miracle if a whale wandered in."

"You sure?"

Bender barks a deep affirmative bark like a bassett hound. Then bays at an imaginary moon. Silver glitter sprinkles onto his black kimono, like stardust, then onto the floor.

This would all be a funny story to tell Carlotta, but when Leon arrives at Lucky's, she isn't there. Neither is Dagmar. Nor Sam, although his new red Firebird is still parked where Leon left it.

They are gone, all of them.

And so, unfortunately, is the American Dream—with all that beautiful chrome and the tiny lavender mouse pillows.

"Yellow is just not my lucky color," Leon says, and it starts to thunder, then rain.

Chapter 32

When Jimmy Ray discovered that his machete was missing, he knew Jesus was coming back. But he didn't bother calling Dagmar, or Mr. Trot. There was really no need. Jimmy Ray felt he could handle this himself.

So, he waits.

Outside his tiny key lime house there are fists of lighting. Jimmy Ray sits in the dark kitchen dressed in a black turtleneck sweater, black trousers, and soft-soled shoes—warrior's clothes— and listens to the cacophony of scanners, the great chatter of humanity. Every now and then a flash of lightning illuminates the room. Then darkness again.

Jimmy Ray feels calm. He prays for wisdom to Buddha and God in equal measure. When the kitchen door finally opens, he is ready.

"I don't understand, son," he says.

A bolt of lightning strikes nearby. For a moment, Jesus is illuminated—his crown-of-thorn scars, the haunted sad eyes. He seems more vulnerable, smaller than Jimmy Ray imagines him to be, but there is blood splattered everywhere—across his face, his bare chest, the shirt wrapped around his waist, and the machete.

"Let's take a ride," Jesus says. "Don't forget to bring your harmonica."

Behind Lucky's RV Round-Up, the beached body of Sam the Gator, former University of Florida football star, rocks back and forth in the waves. Trot's cell phone lies next to it, ringing.

As does Trot. His blood mixes with rain, saltwater.

Chapter 33

The biggest problem with the Nancy Drew "Girl Sleuth" books is that the legions of little girls who read them grew up to be responsible intelligent women who somehow, in the face of unexpected peril, believe that all you need is pluck.

Luckily, at the age of sixteen, Dagmar discovered Ian Fleming's *James Bond*.

So she's at The Dream Café looking for Uncle Joe's gun. She always keeps it in her top drawer, just in case she needs it. It's a Jimmy Cagney tough guy snub-nosed Colt Classic .38.

"It's a short man's gun," Uncle Joe used to say. "Looks like it means business, even if you don't."

But she can't find it. It was in her desk two days ago. It's always in her desk. She remembers seeing it last when Jimmy Ray and Jesus came for Happy Hour. She showed it to them as part of the tour. "My bodyguard," she called it.

"You still got that thing?" Jimmy Ray said.

"Stylish," said Jesus.

That's the very last time she saw it.

Shit, she thinks.

Just then Bernie knocks on the office door and opens it without waiting for an answer. "Thought you'd like to know we're sold out," she says. It's half an hour before the first show. Bernie is dressed like a peacock, with a huge plume of feathers and an iridescent G-string. Her red hair is piled on top of her head. She is Las Vegas beautiful.

This year's New Year's Eve theme is Moulin Rouge— big and glitzy. One hundred dollars per couple for the early bird show. A hundred fifty after 9 P.M. Sold out means about $5,000 net for the first show alone.

Dagmar should be ecstatic, but isn't. She's too worried. "Great," she says, but doesn't look up. She's got to find that gun. She pulls out the top file drawer, shakes it. Papers and files fall into a heap. The office is a mess.

"Anything I can do?" Bernie asks.

"Jimmy Ray call?"

Bernie shakes her head. Her peacock feathers catch the light. Seem to throw tiny rainbows. "Haven't heard from him since the wake.

"It's nice your ex isn't dead, don't you think?"

Dagmar gives Bernie a look that reminds her of a chow

she once had to have put down. "Sorry," Bernie says and closes the door gently behind her.

Dagmar picks up the phone and calls Jimmy Ray again. Still no answer. It's the fourth time in an hour. This isn't good. She starts to call Trot when Bernie opens the door again. Looks sheepish.

"Can I ask a favor?"

"Hurry up," Dagmar says. From the tone of her voice the answer feels like no—no matter what the favor is. So Bernie takes a deep breath, straightens the peacock feathers over her breasts. "Well, here's the deal," she says and then pauses. She's trying to find the right words.

Dagmar taps her watch. "Half an hour to showtime."

"Right. Well, I know how you don't like boyfriends hanging around, but since the bouncer quit—"

"The bouncer quit?"

"Yesterday. Got a better offer in Miami."

"Why doesn't anybody tell me?"

"I left a note just in case you noticed he wasn't here. I figured you'd notice, though. I mean he is like a four-hundred-pound Samoan—"

"Is there a point to this?" Dagmar is hands-on-hips angry, mostly with herself.

"Well, my boyfriend would like to be the bouncer for tonight—"

"No."

"But."

"You know the rules about boyfriends."

"But—"

The door opens wider. Preacher, the trucker from Christmas, the one who traded the Vietnamese prayer for his breakfast, stands next to Bernie.

Bernie is blushing. Shrugs.

Dagmar is certainly surprised. She did not expect this at all.

Preacher is dressed in a tuxedo. He's an odd combination of handsome and menacing. In his large manicured hands he's holding a florist's box with an old-fashioned orchid corsage inside. The tag reads "To: Bernadette."

Jeez, Dagmar thinks.

"I'm sorry to barge in Mrs.," he says. "I don't want to break any rules. If you want me to pay for both shows, I will."

Not dating guests is another rule, Dagmar wants to say, but Bernie has a lot of loyal fans. Doesn't want to lose her.

Still, she thinks, rules are rules.

"Bernie," Dagmar says in that strained way she has, but before she can say anything else, the blushing woman dressed in peacock feathers pulls her aside.

"I know what you're thinking," she whispers quickly, "but the rest of the girls don't know Preacher was a guest. And he's got a good heart—and a good heart is hard to find."

She's nearly pleading. She's in love, Dagmar thinks.

Amazingly, Preacher seems to be blushing, too. "I'm sorry. I don't want to cause any problems," he says. Sounds sheepish, looks hulking—it's all very incongruous.

"Jeez," Dagmar says, giving in. "All right. Preacher, we don't get a lot of trouble here. Mostly we get couples, especially on New Year's Eve. So just fit in. Don't let anybody touch the girls—that's your main concern."

"Yes'm."

"We'll work out the money later."

"I don't need—"

"Well, you'll take it, just in case something happens. I want you to fill out an application form, too. You need to be on staff and covered by insurance—even if it's just for one night."

"Yes'm."

"Bernie, you make sure Preacher gets what he needs."

Then Dagmar turns back to her desk. Picks up the phone again.

"Mrs.?" Preacher interrupts. "Can I just ask you one thing?"

Dagmar taps her watch again. "Twenty-five minutes before showtime."

"Sorry," he says. "It's just . . . could you call me Carl? That's my given name. 'Preacher' is just something the guys call me."

That Buddha heart, Dagmar thinks, there it is again. Jeez. Well, at least somebody has one.

"Carl's a nice name," she says.

"It was my father's."

"Glad to hear it. That's nice. Now, Carl get out of here. Take Bernie with you."

He takes Bernie's hand and they're both goofy, beaming.

Lovesick, Dagmar thinks. "Back to work," she says. "Or I'll fire both your asses."

When the door closes behind them, Dagmar dials Jimmy Ray again. With Jesus missing, she didn't want to leave him alone, but he insisted. "I'm just old, not helpless," he told her. Still, she made him lock the doors. But now the phone rings without answer. *Shit.*

She slams down the receiver just as Bernie runs back into the office and kisses her on the cheek. "Thanks," Bernie whispers.

"Get to work," Dagmar says, as gruff as she can muster. Love, she thinks, what a waste of time. Then she calls Trot's cell. He doesn't answer either.

"Where in the name of hell are you guys?"

It's clear she's going to have to find them, even without a gun.

Just call me Nancy Drew, she thinks—and doesn't like the sound of that at all.

Chapter 34

"**D**o you know any polkas?" Jesus asks.

This is not exactly the question Jimmy Ray expects. "I make it a point as a professional to know a little bit of everything," he says. "But I'm no Frankie Yankovic."

The two men are driving the American Dream down the narrow dirt road that leads to what was once Pettit's Alligator farm, although Jesus doesn't know that. He just knows it's the main road in town, and it leads out toward the peninsula he saw earlier—and it's deserted. Deserted is a good quality in a road.

"I love Yankovic," Jesus says, as if they're just

out for a drive. "A lot of people don't know that he isn't Polish at all."

This is more than Jimmy Ray ever wanted or expected to know about America's Polka King.

"Can you sing me a little?" Jesus asks.

Jimmy Ray gives him an incredulous look. "Sing you a little *polka*? You brought me out here in this storm to sing *polka songs*?"

"Well, no. But I think it would make the experience a little more pleasant for us both."

"You're fixing to kill me, but first you want a musical interlude?"

Jesus turns to Jimmy Ray, looks sheepish. "Well, you didn't have to bring your harmonica, just because I told you to."

"You had a machete."

"I was just holding it," Jesus shrugs. "Wasn't trying to scare you."

When he says this he no longer looks menacing, just tired and dirty. Looks like Jimmy Ray's friend again—just a little bit more lost, and a little less harmless. Jimmy Ray softens.

That's some kind of crazy you got going on, he thinks and can't imagine the struggle inside the man's head.

"Well," Jimmy Ray says, "no musician can resist a willing audience."

Jesus smiles. Jimmy Ray takes the harmonica and riffs a classic blues-based two-step beat. "Roll out the barrel," he growls. "You gots to roll out that little barrel baby 'cause I'm your handyman."

Unfortunately, the polka loses a lot in translation.

When they finally arrive at the end of the road, Jesus guns the engine. What little gas the Dream has left in it propels it through the passion fruit flower archway. Then it stalls.

In the clearing sits the ghost house.

"Shoot," Jimmy Ray says, amazed.

The electrical storm is raging around them. White-capped waves surround the small house. The gigantic gator grin, an entrance like no other, rocks in the high wind.

"What's this?" Jesus asks.

"A miracle," Jimmy Ray says.

At that moment, on the dirt road that connects Whale Harbor to the interstate and the rest of the world, Dagmar is officially going twice the posted speed limit. The rain is sheeting down, makes the road fluid around her. The Mercedes is well designed, able to go 100 mph on the Autobahn.

This, however, is not the Autobahn.

Going 50 mph she hydroplanes but has the presence of mind to take her foot off the gas and downshift. The small convertible spins like a bottle in the center of the road. The car is heavy so it doesn't flip.

Lucky, she thinks right before her head hits the steering wheel.

Leon is also feeling lucky, but not entirely happy about it. He's sitting alone in the parking lot of the Round-Up in his mandarin orange 1975 El Dorado looking at himself in the rearview mirror. "Rancid Creamsicle. That's what I look like. A big friggin' rancid Creamsicle." The shrink-wrapped money is in the trunk. Bob the Round-Up Cowboy is wantonly tossing his lasso in the blinding rain.

Life is good. Leon knows he should be happy. He has every reason to be happy. If he leaves right now, he can be in Miami in three hours. He can rent a room at one of those pink hotels and drink imported beer. Maybe even watch wrestling on the pay-per-view channel. With a big bag of shrink-wrapped cash, you can even eat the macadamia nuts from the tiny locked refrigerator. Life, at the moment, is filled with possibilities. There really is nothing to keep Leon in Whale Harbor anymore. No women. No family. He can sell Grammy Lettie's house—since there really is a house to sell now. Sell Lucky's. Start a new life. And he knows he can, and should, do this because as soon as Trot discovers that there was a big bag of money taped to the bottom of the Posture-Perfect, he's going to be pissed—and that's never good.

So Leon knows what he really needs to do is put the car in reverse, back out of Lucky's parking lot, and never look back. He turns the key in the ignition. The windshield wipers slap on. The headlights waver in the rain. He checks the rearview mirror again.

"I still look like a friggin' rancid Creamsicle." Then he throws it in reverse. But instead of pulling away, he idles. The engine rumbles, bucks.

That kid is missing.

And so is Dr. Ricky Jesus.

And the money has to belong to that Levi couple. They owned the Dream. They have to be dead.

These are not my problems, he tells himself, and the engine whines.

Then, unfortunately, he thinks about all the people who came to him when he was Bee-Jesus. They all wanted him to save them, but he couldn't. Never could save anybody, he thinks. Not Miss Pearl, the Amazing One-Ton Wonder. Not Grandma Lettie. Not even my own boy, Cal.

When he thinks of his son, Leon remembers that awful look of panic on Cal's sweet face as the water pulled him down. The memory feels so real, Leon can't catch his breath; feels as if he's drowning in it.

Not even myself, he thinks. I can't even save myself. And he feels beyond sorrow, all tapped out. So Leon pulls out of the parking lot and starts down the long dirt road that used to be paved, used to have a sign that welcomed visitors to Whale Harbor. He heads in the blinding rain toward the interstate and the world beyond. No reason to stay, every reason to leave. Time to start over. Get a new life.

But then, about a mile down the road, he sees Dagmar, bruised and bleeding, waving him down in the sheeting rain. Her tiny sea green convertible blocks the road. He has to stop. So he does. He opens the car door to let her in. He plans to explain that he's leaving, starting over. There's nothing left for me here anymore, he wants to say.

But the dome light makes her face seem even more beautiful. Soft as magnolias.

"That Jesus guy got Jimmy Ray," she says.

She's dripping all over the mandarin orange leather of

the Pimp Daddy Caddy. "I'm pretty sure of it. I think he's going to kill him."

That's when Leon notices it. He can't believe he never noticed it before. In the soft moon of the dome light, Dagmar's eyes—they're Cal's eyes with those tiny specks of green and gold.

Our son, he thinks. Then leans over and kisses her hard.

Dagmar's stunned. So is Leon.

"Let's go kick some psycho butt," he says and throws the Pimp Daddy Caddy into reverse.

For once in her life, Dagmar is speechless.

Chapter 35

Bleeding to death is not an unpleasant experience, except for that moment of sheer panic when you realize it's going to happen, and you're helpless to stop it, and you don't want to die so your heart races, beats against the bone of your chest, and you'd like to scream but you can't.

Other than that, it's really quite a lovely way to go.

Of course, as the blood leaves your hands and feet the cold becomes difficult. But then, luckily, when the blood slips away from the brain you lose consciousness. Then die.

Except for the mess, it's all rather pleasant.

"You're not giving up this easy, Trot Jeeter."

The sweet voice pulls him back into life. He opens his eyes.

"That's good," Carlotta says. "You look at me. You stay awake."

She's elevated Trot's head and applied pressure so that the bleeding has slowed. "They trained all the dealers at the casino in first aid," she says. "I know what I'm doing. Just do what I tell you. Just look at me. Nowhere else."

Even if I die, this is my lucky day, he thinks.

"Can you hear me? Can you wink at me?"

Definitely lucky.

The rain is coming down horizontal. Hard. Stings the skin. The smell of dead fish is overwhelming. The waves crash over them. Carlotta holds Trot close. She has to keep him awake and his head above water. Has to keep him focused, alert. Has to make sure they both don't drown.

She's trying hard not to panic, but it's difficult. Sam's lifeless body is rocking back and forth next to her. It's half on shore, half still afloat. Every now and then, a wave carries the dead boy's hand and it brushes up against her back. Or her leg. Or arm.

It's so cold, lifeless. She wants to scream, but can't. Can't upset Trot. Can't risk it. Can't move him either. His skin is already clammy. Blood seems to be everywhere. Pressure must be maintained—she knows that.

When the dead boy's hand comes to rest on her thigh, his dull fat fingers, she takes a sharp breath. Feels the acid in her stomach rise. Focuses on Trot.

"You'll be fine," she says in that voice that's an odd mix of steel and silk. "I called for backup on your cell. They'll be here soon."

With each wave, Sam's fingers seem to move back and forth over her thigh. Caress it. It's difficult not to scream.

"You got to hold on," she says to Trot. "Hold on tight."

He wants to smile, but can't manage it. Things are murky. He's not sure what happened. All he remembers is that Jesus had the boy. He doesn't remember drawing his gun. Doesn't remember Jesus saying, "You believe in salvation?" Doesn't remember the machete, or Carlotta finding him.

A wave crashes over them both and makes her cough so hard she nearly loses her grip on him. "You're lucky I like the beach," she says.

"You make me want cotton candy," Trot whispers.

Or at least thinks he does.

Chapter 36

Jesus never could resist a good miracle.

"Miracle house? That should be interesting," he says, as if he's just another tourist planning his day. "I'll clean up and we'll take a quick look. It'll be fun."

Jimmy Ray says nothing. He stares out the window into the night and can see the whitecaps of high waves illuminated by lightning as they overwhelm the small house. He picks up the harmonica and plays an old Underground Railroad song. "Wade in the Water"—"God is gonna trouble the water."

Gives him strength. Hope.

Jesus hums along as he takes the top bed sheet

off the king-sized Posture-Perfect and wraps it around his bony waist. He washes his face in the tiny marble sink with the small pink shell soaps that Mrs. Levi had bought to match the towels. Then tidies up the machete.

"Mistake," the voices in his head whisper. "You're making a big mistake."

But he ignores them. How often does one get to see a miracle?

When he's finished he says, "Presentable?" There are still traces of blood deep in the creases of his face.

"Somewhat," Jimmy Ray says and looks away. How'd you get so wrong? he thinks and looks back out the window. The night is so dark it feels as if he'll be swallowed up by it. The anger of the storm is the only light. The ghost house sits in the middle of this fury, its silvered timber dulled.

"Doesn't look like anybody's at home," Jimmy Ray says.

"That's all right. We'll just take a quick look around."

When Jesus passes through the tiny kitchen he blows out the pilot light of the oven. Turns up the gas. The smell is suddenly overwhelming. "This will take awhile, anyway," he says.

Jimmy Ray is clearly alarmed. "You figuring on killing me in this thing?"

Jesus smiles, proud. "It's the Hallmark card of death, don't you think? Killed by the American Dream—how perfect a death is that for a Buddhist?"

Jimmy Ray shakes his head, sadly. "I don't know, son. Exploding like that sort of fit Leon, but it seems a little too flashy for me."

"Oh, I'm not blowing you up. That would be gaudy. Carbon monoxide is so much more thoughtful. The silent killer."

"Makes you ralph, I've heard."

Jesus is clearly disappointed in his friend. "You're going to be fussy, aren't you? You promised me you weren't fussy. And now, here you are, being fussy." He picks up a flashlight from on top of the tiny refrigerator. "Salvation is never easy," he says to himself and the two men run out into the cresting storm, Jesus swinging the machete over his head like a majorette at halftime; Jimmy Ray two steps behind.

It'll be okay, Jimmy Ray tells himself. The rain chills his skin. Uncle Joe's snub-nosed Colt Classic .38 bulges in his pant pocket. I can handle this. As he runs, he sings in his rumble of a voice, "Wade in the water. Wade in the water, children. Wade in the water. God's a-going to trouble the water."

Luckily, help is on the way. More or less. The Pimp Daddy Caddy tires are nearly bald, so the mandarin orange car is weaving through the quickly flooding town like a wayward ocean liner. But at least it's moving and going in the right direction. Since there's only one paved road in Whale Harbor, Leon knows that there's really only one place to go with a $250,000 land yacht that is nearly out of fuel.

It's a no-brainer even for me, he thinks. But he doesn't want to think much more beyond that. Thinking always seems to get him into trouble. He knows that if he thinks too much, he'll soon convince himself that he should be afraid, and then he'll chicken out. So he just thinks about baseball. He has to, because he has no idea what they're going to do when they find Jesus and Jimmy Ray. He has no plan, no weapon, and borrowed courage.

I'm in my element when I'm in over my head, he reassures himself. Then wonders if the Marlins will ever make the World Series.

When they finally arrive at the end of the road, the Dream is dark. He parks a little way down from it. "They're probably in the house," he says. Then turns the dome light on again quickly. Just one more look, he thinks. For courage.

Dagmar turns to him and finally speaks. "Thanks," she says, and he hears Cal's voice.

"Anytime."

Inside the house, Jesus and Jimmy Ray are sitting at the kitchen table waiting for the rain to stop. Jesus takes the flashlight and turns it on. Balances it on the table. The light points toward the ceiling, and fills the room with a burnished glow, as if the moment is already a memory.

"Maybe we could just talk," Jesus says. "To pass the time. Wait for the rain to let up." He's going to miss Jimmy Ray; he knows that now. Miss him a lot.

This is the mistake, the voices inside Jesus' head say. No talking. Never talk.

"I'm not ready for salvation," Jimmy Ray says.

THIS IS WHY YOU SHOULD NEVER TALK, the voices scream. Jesus understands now. Talking always leads to confusion. "Sorry," he says under his breath.

"You okay?" Jimmy Ray says.

Jesus nods.

"I hope you understand what I'm saying," Jimmy Ray says. "It's not that I don't appreciate the gesture—"

Jesus raises his hand to silence him. "Maybe we should stop talking."

Salvation is a gift, Jesus wants to say, and not accepting a gift is rude. But he doesn't say this. Even thinking about rudeness makes him angry. He doesn't want to be angry with Jimmy Ray. He wants to be gentle. "We can just sit here quietly. That's okay."

"I'm not trying to upset you," Jimmy Ray says. "I just think you should know that I've thought about it and I'm not ready to go. Not yet. What I'm ready to do is to go back to New Orleans and take me a job at Preservation Hall; I know some of the boys there. And then I plan to find me a fine-looking widow with a solid pension who knows how to cook and still has most of her own teeth.

"You see I still got some living yet. You made me see that."

"But the American Dream," Jesus sighs, wistful. "Such a mythic death."

"Son, don't get me wrong. I appreciate the beauty of it and celebrate its metaphoric qualities. It's genius."

"You're not just saying that?"

Jimmy Ray shakes his head. "No, sir. I am touched that you honor me with such a death."

"But—"

"Well—"

"Then you're going to have to kill me," Jesus says, "because I have planned your salvation, and am counting on your salvation, and I will have your salvation.

"The only way you're going to go on living is over my dead body.

"Do you think you can do that? Kill me?"

Jesus places the machete on the table between them, within arm's reach of them both. The kitchen provides uneasy shelter. The wind outside is off-key and raging. The surf crashes up against the small house like a drunk. Saltwater flows though the worn walls. Rain sheets through the glassless windows. The two men cannot look into each other's eyes, but have no choice.

Neither is sure what they see.

"Forgiveness," Jimmy Ray says. "I can forgive you and you can forgive me. And we can both walk away. You know, Buddha says there can be no true healing without forgiveness of ourselves and of others."

Jesus nods and thinks about it for a moment. Then he says, "But if you're planning on getting out of here alive, I'd grab the machete, if I were you. The Colt has no bullets."

Jimmy Ray isn't sure that he heard that right. "What do you mean? What Colt?"

"I know you have it. Go on, take a look at it," Jesus says. "I wouldn't lie to you. I'm a lot of things, but I'm not a liar. Go ahead."

Jimmy Ray slowly takes the gun from his pants pocket. Checks it. Empty.

"I took them out," Jesus says. "When you slipped away

that night after your set at The Café, it was easy to figure out where you were. When you were asleep, I removed the bullets."

"How'd you know I wouldn't check the gun again?"

"Buddhist. Bad enough you have the gun."

"I see."

Jimmy Ray puts the gun back into his pocket. Who am I fooling? he thinks. I am too old for this. Living has slipped through my hands.

Jesus can feel the shift in him, the weakness. Jimmy Ray's skin seems suddenly like an overcoat worn slack. The old man eyes are back, weak and watery. Jesus plays his hand again. "You know you won't kill me. And it's not because of some moral compass you have. It's because you don't want to. You know I'm right. It is time for you to go.

"This world, Jimmy Ray, is no place for a noble spirit like you. There's just too much sorrow."

Jimmy Ray goes quiet. He counts his dead as one would sheep. After a time he says, "Sorrow's the one thing we can be sure of in this world. That's why we got to make joy." But when he says this, he doesn't sound convinced. It's clear he's struggling. He wants to believe, but isn't sure if he really does.

Jesus feels the bluff, and goes "all-in." "But you know what they say," he says, seductive. "Bowlers bowl—you can't change the nature of the world, Jimmy Ray. Sorrow grows in your bones."

Time suddenly feels slowed. Jesus reaches across and

hands Jimmy Ray the machete. Pushes the table over. The two men sit knee to knee.

"So kill me, or let me kill you," Jesus whispers. The voices in his head go silent.

Jimmy Ray looks at the long sharp blade, and then at Jesus. "I'm not going to kill you, son."

"But you brought that gun."

"To talk sense into you."

"Still, you brought the gun. And the Luger before that. Not exactly Buddhist."

The words settle in. Itch. Jimmy Ray shrugs.

Jesus smiles. "Doesn't mean you're not a good man. You brought the gun because we both know that sometimes a life just isn't worth living anymore.

"Takes a real friend to give the gift of salvation. And you want that gift, now. I know you do. I can feel it."

Jimmy Ray's knees shake slightly with the weight of the knife.

"I could take you back to the Dream," Jesus says, "and let you lie on the satin sheets and you could live again that life you always sing about—all smoke and whiskey and big-lipped women reckless as Saturday night—not widows with their clacking teeth, but young women with smooth fine fur who will roll you between their legs until you are speechless and they will be all yours forever as you fall into that white hot moment of death and slip from this world to the next.

"I can do that for you because we're friends."

Outside, the rain grows soft. The waves, slack. The storm is lifting. The world is suddenly too quiet.

"It would be a death fitting your great spirit," Jesus says. "A death that will be remembered. A death that should not go to waste."

The words pain the old man, because he feels the truth in them. "I'm sorry," he says and reaches across and pats Jesus' shoulder. "But I can't let you do that, son."

"Then kill me," Jesus says.

At this moment, timing is everything. And Leon knows it. But that's about all he knows. All he wants to know. "Don't think!" he shouts and crashes through the kitchen door.

Of course, the best part about not thinking is that you have no way to judge the rightness of your actions. No censoring that informs you as to whether an idea is hare-brained, or absurd, or too dangerous—or just plain stupid.

It is for this reason why heroes fall into two categories—the fearless and the morons.

So when Leon crashes through the kitchen door, a blur of color in his borrowed crime scene yellow and hemoglobin clothes, screaming "Don't think! Don't think! Don't think!" as he tackles Jesus from behind sending the chair and the man careening into Jimmy Ray and knocking the machete out of his lap and onto the floor so that Jesus could swoop it up and say, "I'll miss you. You were a good friend," and then run out the door of the ghost house into the cold sweat of the night—Dagmar pretty much decides that Leon is one of the few men on earth who actually fits into both categories.

Leon is, indeed, the bravest and most stupid man she has ever met.

"You okay?" she asks Jimmy Ray, holds him close. He nods, shaky.

Leon helps him up. "I guess I saved you," he says, shocked. "I've never saved anybody before."

"I guess you did," Jimmy says sadly.

And at that moment, $250,000 of American engineering and buyable luxury explodes.

The American Dream killed Jesus. Of course, he lit the match.

Chapter 37

The story Harlan Oakley wrote for the *National Examiner* was not titled "The Next Refrigerator Perry Asks Jesus for a Leg Up," as Sam thought it would be. Instead, "Killer on Rampage" was splashed across page one.

Sam the Gator Boy was remembered fondly as a large angry child filled with promise who was never quite lucky enough. Harlan wept as he wrote it. The *Examiner* ran it straight. No Photoshopped pictures of Jesus being abducted by aliens, just an all-American shot of Sam in his University of Florida football uniform, full of hope and dreams.

Because of the story people came to Whale

Harbor once more. Not just the media with their live shots and TV tans, but visitors. Everyone wanted to travel the murderer's trail. They wanted to see where Sam's body washed ashore.

Some even thought they saw whales.

The town slowly began to come back to life. The Pink was suddenly crowded at lunch. Bender dyed his hair a tarnished spoon platinum. He finally settled on Weimaraner as his inner dog and now thanks customers with an aristocratic silver bark. Mrs. Sitwell opened a Kettle Korn stand.

As the story of Sam spread, those who called themselves "Believers" came to pray for his soul. A group of Evangelicals even set up a tent and a gospel mission outside The Dream Café. Now, daily, they give the dancers comfortable shoes with Bible quotes written in them and ask them to repent. The minister has tied himself to a cross that he planted under the sign that reads, "Naughty but Nice!" He's wearing a rainbow-colored umbrella hat to ward off the sun. His hands are bound to the wood with Velcro, as are his feet. "Just in case he has to tinkle," his wife tells the press. It's a great photo opportunity, but not so great for business.

So when Leon drives up in his mandarin orange Pimp Daddy Caddy, the place is nearly deserted. Dagmar is sitting on a folding chair watching potential customers make U-turns out of the driveway. Leon hasn't seen her for nearly a month, ever since he saved Jimmy Ray. So much has changed since then.

Leon has moved into Grammy Lettie's, mostly for crowd control, at least that's what he says. But at night he sits in the dark kitchen and remembers the days when he was a boy, when Whale Harbor was a real town, and Miss Pearl was his best girl.

Howdy.

He thinks about the idea of opening Pettit's again. He still has that shrink-wrapped bag of the Levis' money—nobody ever asked after it. So he has the capital. But he wants to spend it right. The money feels like a second chance. He doesn't want to blow it.

If he reopens Pettit's, he knows it can't be the way it used to be. Got to be something classy. Got to be something that lets the wild cats play on the beach, and lets the peacocks screech, and the fat manatees, with their stuffed toy smiles, play tag in the bright green water. But Leon has no idea how all these things can happen at a first-rate tourist attraction. And he has no one to ask. Carlotta has moved on.

So much has changed, he thinks, except for Dagmar. As he parks the Pimp Daddy Caddy he can see that she is still every inch the Egyptian queen. It took him a month to get his courage up to stop by to see her. His hands shake. He stuffs them in his pockets.

"Hey," he says.

"Hey."

He watches along with her for a while as if the line of deserting customers is some sort of a parade.

"Pretty soon," he says. "Things will get back to normal."

"I hope not," she says. "I've decided to franchise, and then go public. Use the publicity, and the national exposure, as a marketing push.

"As Jimmy Ray says, 'It's all good.'"

"You miss him?"

Dagmar shrugs. "New Orleans isn't that far away."

Leon sits in the chair next to her. "So what do you know about running a first-rate tourist attraction?"

She looks at him, honey-eyed, and laughs. "More than you do."

"I guess that's the story of our lives."

He reaches his hand out to her, and she takes it.

"I guess it is," she says.

Chapter 38

Trot and Carlotta are in his boat trolling the shoreline. Not fishing, just watching the sun set. Trot's still sore, taped up tight, but happy. The horizon, which he's seen so many times on his own, is turning that particular shade of pink that only can be found in this part of the world. As the fading light spreads, it washes over them. Turns their skin blush.

"Flamingos," she says. "The belly of conch shells. Hibiscus."

"Pepto-Bismol?"

"I can see that."

Trot can't help but grin. The waves lap up against the boat, gently rock it back and forth.

"Now what?" she says and leans into him slightly. With her hair piled onto her head and the delicate lace of her scar, she is more beautiful than any one woman has a right to be. So Trot tells her the story of Hurricane Donna. It's the most romantic thing he can think of.

"My grandpa Buck was mayor at the time. He was well into his seventies, lean as driftwood. Grammy Jules, his twin.

"The thing was, nobody thought Donna would be that bad," he says. Trot's never told this story to any woman before—not even Dagmar. Unfortunately, the best part of it he doesn't know. It's long dead.

As Hurricane Donna approached there was something about the low sky, bruise green and churning, that made Buck and Jules feel uneasy. But the roads were washed away. They couldn't leave.

"Don't matter now," Jules whispered. Her voice was smoky like it was when they first met, and they were still a mystery to each other.

As Donna neared, the two made love in their own bed with slowness that comes not from age, but deep pleasure. And knowing.

And when they were through, Buck and Jules moved into a large pantry near the center of the house. A safe place. At the first word of the storm, Jules had taken all her orchids from under the orange trees and placed them there. In the dark room, surrounded by dozens of orchids and their gentle sweet perfume, Old Buck and Jules fell in and out of an uneasy sleep. Kissed every now and then, just because.

The rest of the story, everyone knows.

Hurricane Donna finally lumbered ashore around midnight. Her surge was enormous, several stories high. When she hit Old Buck and Jules' tiny bungalow the roof lifted. The harbor poured in over the walls and overflowed the house like a bucket. Furniture. Orchids. Everything gone in one great wave. Old Buck grabbed for Jules and caught her by the hair.

"One thing I learned through forty-seven years of marriage," he later said, "you hang on to each other no matter what. You don't let go."

"Grandpa Buck rode the surge into town," Trot tells Carlotta. "Swam the flooded streets for hours. Too tough to drown, some said. Probably was true.

"When he was finally rescued, dehydrated, delirious, he thought Grammy Jules was still there. He held wisps of long gray hair tightly in his fist. Wouldn't let go.

"'Forty-seven years,' he said over and over again until he grew hoarse."

Trot took a deep breath. The story overwhelmed him.

"Till death do you part," Carlotta says.

"Grandpa Buck never really got over it. Threw himself into the harbor and drowned on the first anniversary of the storm. 'Missing Jules,' the note read."

Trot's voice cracks when he says this. He falls silent.

"That's a wonderful story. Thank you," Carlotta says softly. Bites her lip. Doesn't want to cry.

"Ever been married?" he asks.

She shrugs. "Not like that. What about you?"

Trot shakes his head. His hand moves to his chest, to the wound.

"I've been waiting for a woman who won't let go," he says, and Carlotta remembers sitting in the surf with him—remembers the prayers she prayed, the promises she made to a god she seldom believed in—so she leans over and kisses him.

Cherry pie, he thinks.

In the distance, well beyond them, in the fading fuchsia of the sky, there is an amazing sight.

Whale.

A real whale. A lost "firecracker," as they're called in Japan. Also known as "pygmy." Its belly is filled with crab and squid. Happy, it lies on top of the waves, floating, bobbing. Its gray skin reflects the sky, turns the color of roses. When its mate finally catches up, the two dive underwater, somersaulting around each other. Playful.

As the sun extinguishes into the Gulf, and the world goes dark again, the firecrackers break through the surface of the water and blow ink into the sky like a *tsunabi,* as the Japanese fisherman say, a rocketing firework.

They are twin fireworks against the darkness of night.

But Trot and Carlotta don't notice.

Novelist N. M. KELBY is also the author of *In the Company of Angels* and *Theater of the Stars.* She spent more than twenty years as a print and television journalist before she began writing. Her poems and short stories have appeared in more than fifty journals including *Zoetrope All-Story Extra, One Story, Southeast Review,* and *The Mississippi Review.* She is the recipient of a Bush Artist Fellowship in Literature, the Heekin Group Foundation's James Fellowship for the Novel, both a Florida and Minnesota State Arts Board Fellowship in fiction, two Jerome Travel Study Grants, and a Jewish Arts Endowment Fellowship. She grew up in Florida, where she currently lives. Her website is www.nmkelby.com.

TELL THE WORLD THIS BOOK WAS

GOOD	BAD	SO-SO

A NOTE ON THE TYPE

The text of this book was set in Perrywood MT, a typeface designed in 1993 by Johannes Birkenback (b. 1956) for the Monotype Corporation. Influenced by Bembo and Plantin, Perrywood is a successful attempt to wed the charm of old style, hot metal letterforms with the regularities of digital fonts. Initially released with just five weights, Perrywood has grown to a family of thirty.